Pieces of Her

BEING A WOMAN IS NOT FOR THE FAINT OF HEART

A SHORT STORY COLLECTION

To Sarah,

BARBARA V. EVERS

Stay strong!

BV Evers

CAMELEOPARD PRESS

Published in the United States by Cameleopard Press, an imprint of VL Publishing

Greer, SC

Print ISBN: 978-1-959859-04-8

Ebook ISBN: 978-1-959859-05-5

This book is dedicated to the memory of my mother who taught me how to be a lady and to the many women who have inspired me ever since.

Acknowledgments

"Prayers for Bethany" first appeared in *The Petigru Review, Vol 9,* published by South Carolina Writers' Workshop, 2015.

"Cedar Revenge" first appeared in *The Petigru Review, Vol 12,* published by South Carolina Writers' Association, 2018.

"John-E-Mail" first appeared in *The Petigru Review, Vol 8,* published by South Carolina Writers' Workshop, 2014

"Just Me" first appeared in the *moonShine review, Vol 12, Issue 2* published by moonSHINE Review Press, 2016.

"The Wall" first appeared in the *moonShine review, Vol 15, Issue 2* published by moonSHINE Review Press, 2019.

"Pieces" first appeared in the *moonShine review, Vol 9, Issue 1,* published by moonSHINE Review Press, 2013.

"The Devil's Wife" first appeared in the *moonShine review, Vol 10,* published by moonSHINE Review Press, 2013.

"Gentle Snow" first appeared in the *moonShine review, Vol 9, Issue 2,* published by moonSHINE Review Press, 2013.

Cover art ©Chainat|Dreamstime.com File ID 174987820

Contents

Prayers for Bethany

The minutes ticked by in agonizing eons, drop by drop in time with the saving liquid in the IV bag hung by Bethany's bed in the ICU. Jane, her mother, stared at the fluid wondering how it helped, if it helped, her daughter. The young girl lay on the bed, still and quiet as death, her skin paler than the white sheets hiding most of her injuries.

The steady beep of a machine rang in Jane's ears. A glance at the clock told her only ten minutes had passed since the last time she'd checked, but she couldn't help herself. Never, in a million years, had she expected to sit by the bedside of her one and only child watching life play a game of hide and seek.

She stood and smoothed the hair back from her daughter's forehead, one of the few spots unmarred from the accident. Bob had gone to the crash site and to the junk yard to see the car, the one that boy drove off the road and rolled, her daughter's body bouncing like a rag doll with each screeching impact of metal against ground.

"Mrs. Albright?" A nurse in teddy-bear-covered smocks stood in the doorway. "I need to change her bandages. Why don't you get something from the cafeteria? It will take me a while."

Jane heard the unspoken words.

You don't want to see these injuries, the damage done to your daughter's arms, legs, her soft belly where Jane gave her zerberts as a baby. Her back, shattered, the skin scraped from the surface.

No. She wasn't ready to see those things. Not yet. Not ever. She wasn't ready for any of this.

She kissed Bethany's perfect skin in the only safe spot and whispered, "Courage, Bethie, courage. I need you to stay with me."

The smell of blood, of wounds, assaulted Jane's nose in that brief moment. She backed away breathing deep, filling her nostrils with the antiseptic and medicinal scents of the hospital. Tears threatened, but she blinked them away with each step backward, her tennis shoes squeaking on the polished floor.

At the door, she turned and fled down the hall, barreling through the ICU double doors. She fast-walked past rooms of families dealing with their own crises. She didn't want to know. She didn't want to be there. She wanted to turn back the clock and never see this place.

At the elevator banks she stood as the bell chimed announcing the approach of the moving box. When the doors swooshed open, she stepped back, making room for a CNA pushing a gurney carrying a toddler. The child laughed at something, startling Jane out of her reverie. The doors dinged shut without admitting her.

Jane chewed her lip and stared after the child on the gurney. She sagged against the wall, her purse thumping to the floor. What could she do?

They hadn't known about the boy. Bethany didn't tell them about him. She got in his car, and ...

A buzzing sound harassed her, stinging her ankle, until Jane recognized her phone's vibrations. The distance to the phone in her purse on the floor stretched below her, and she struggled to maintain her balance as she leaned sideways, yanked open the flap of her bag, and fished around for the insistent rectangle still zapping her leg through the leather sides of her purse. She slid her finger over the screen and placed the cool plastic to her ear. "Hello."

Silence.

"Hello?"

More Silence.

A quick glance at the phone's screen revealed a missed call message, the number unfamiliar. While she stared at it, the phone buzzed again, announcing a voice mail. Jane slid her finger over the screen and opened the voicemail app. Sixteen messages? She shoved the phone to the bottom of her purse and straightened the strap on her shoulder. With a firm grip on her bag, she jabbed the lit elevator button and jumped when the doors dinged open.

Inside, she turned to choose a floor, but an elderly man beat her to it. "Where to?" he asked.

"Um?"

Where was the cafeteria? Did she want to go there?

An expression of sympathy crossed the man's face. "First day?"

She jerked her head down, the best she could do to nod.

"How about the coffee shop?" He bent toward her. "They have sandwiches and much better food than the cafeteria."

"Yes," she said. "Thanks."

Caffeine. The thought alone created a surge of desire in her veins. She had abstained for months, warned by her doctor, but today wasn't a normal day.

When the elevator settled to a stop and the doors parted, the man stepped back and gestured her forward. "After you."

Back straight, with quick footsteps, Jane exited the elevator but glanced around in confusion. Where was the coffee shop?

"This way," the man said. "I'm in need of coffee, too." He led her through more double doors and down a hallway that looked familiar. Most of the people in this part of the hospital looked like her. Like they didn't belong. They wore regular clothes. Some stood close, in a huddle. Others stared into space, their hands shoved in their pockets, shoulders hunched to ward off reality. A whiff of cologne streamed from an elderly woman, the stale stink of cigarettes off of a rugged-looking couple. Over it all, she still smelled the medicine, Bethany's wounds, and coffee. The rich aroma grew and blanketed her as the man ushered her through a glass door near the main entrance to the hospital.

"Why don't you sit and let me get this for you?" he said, pulling a chair out for her.

Jane obeyed. "Coffee, black."

"A sandwich maybe? They have good egg salad."

She frowned. Hunger was the least of her concerns. "No," she said. As he turned away, she remembered her manners. "Thank you."

A brief sideways nod acknowledged he had heard her.

While he ordered her coffee, Jane studied the man. He stood about Bob's height, so just under six feet, a halo of white hair rimming his scalp. The deep wrinkles around his eyes proclaimed him older. The man held his shoulders with the ease of someone comfortable with who he was, aware of his purpose in life. Jane had stood with the same stance just yesterday.

"Here you go." He placed a white mug of black coffee in front of her. She wrapped her hands around the ceramic, letting the heat seep into her fingers.

"May I?" He stood beside a chair, his hand hesitating before pulling it out.

"Please." She forced a small smile. "Thank you for helping me."

The man sipped from his cup. A small tassel from a tea bag dangled over the edge. "No problem. We all must help each other when we can." His brown eyes studied her as he placed the cup on the table. "You looked like you needed it."

Uncomfortable with his intent gaze, she looked into the deep swirl of coffee, picked up the cup, and sipped again.

Her manners nudged her, and she asked, "Do you have someone here, too?"

It was his turn to look down. A flash of pain crossed his face. It remained in his eyes as he looked back up at her. "I did."

"Oh." Jane's heart gave a strong beat of agony. In his pain, this man took care of her. She should have done this for him, not the other way around. She reached for his hand, covering it with her own. His skin, wrinkled with age, felt soft under her carefully manicured hands.

"I'm sorry."

"Thank you." He sipped again. "You?"

"My daughter. She's sixteen."

"So young," he said. His confident shoulders sagged under the weight of his world and hers added to it.

"Yes."

They sat for a moment, each tracing patterns over the handles of their cups, neither drinking. Jane glanced at her watch. Somehow, the minutes had passed. The nurse should be done with the bandages by the time she returned to ICU.

He caught her glance. "Time to go back?"

Jane bit her lip. It was nice to sit with someone quietly. Bob had tried, but his anger at the boy boiled around the room making Jane anxious. Finally, she had told Bob to go home, get some rest, do some work. His face looked relieved as he left.

But this man, in the midst of his own pain, a man she didn't even know, gave her the peace she needed.

"They have a chapel on this floor," he said. "I was headed there when I saw you. Would you like to join me?"

Jane smiled at his understanding. "Yes. Please." She reached for her purse. "How much do I owe you?"

"Nothing." He waved her offer away. "If you're a praying woman, maybe you'll pray for my son?"

"You lost him?" Her heart ached with the knowledge of how this must hurt, how close she stood to losing her own child.

"Oh no. No." The man sighed. "He lost his son. My grandson."

Words didn't come to her. She brushed his hand again in sympathy.

They ambled along to the chapel, neither speaking.

The doors swung open to a dimly lit room. An aisle ran down the middle of five rows of pews. Candles burned on an altar, a huge Bible opened between them. Jane slid into a hard pew and folded her hands in her lap. "What is your son's name?"

The man didn't answer. He had approached the altar and stood before the Bible his arms held toward the heavens. He prayed in a soft, but firm voice that echoed in the chamber. "Father, my heart aches, it cracks under the pressure. Please, comfort my son, Jonah. Help him through this loss. And, please embrace our Keith in your arms. Welcome him home to heaven. I pray that my Linda is there to show him your kingdom and to ease his fears."

There was a pause as the man's shoulders heaved. His voice cracked and for a moment, he gave a wordless cry that drove deep into the core of Jane's soul. She bit her lip as tears welled in her eyes.

Ashamed at eavesdropping, Jane bowed her head to pray.

The man spoke again, his voice an urgent whisper. "And God, please, please heal the little girl in Keith's car. Please God, I pray for Bethany."

Cedar Revenge

Heather shivered from the cold as she juggled Mandy in her arms and attempted to unlock the trailer's door. Behind her, Jonah, her husband, stomped his feet on the concrete step, his not-so-subtle way of urging her to hurry. The door swung open, and she scurried inside the small entryway.

"Brrr, it's cold out there." She rubbed chilly noses with her daughter before setting her down.

"Pretty." Mandy's chubby fingers pointed toward the Christmas tree. At fourteen months, the child loved this sparkly addition to their home, staring enthralled at it for long periods of time.

The zipper on the toddler's pink, quilted coat snagged, but Heather finally got it moving and slipped the coat off the child's shoulders.

"Pretty," Mandy said again, but now she pointed at the light on an end table next to their second-hand couch.

Heather glanced up and gasped. A tiny army of bugs streamed up the lamp's base, headed toward the lightbulb. "Jonah, look."

Her husband shook out his coat and turned toward her. "What?" his tone sharp with impatience. The frown creasing his brow shifted toward curiosity, then disgust. "What's that?"

Shuddering with a different chill, Mandy shook her head.

Hundreds of tiny insects streamed in single file lines toward every light in the room. As the baby toddled toward the infantry lines, Heather grabbed her up and rushed down the hallway, checking for more bugs as she went. She flicked on the nursery light and breathed a sigh of relief to find the room bug free.

"Here, play with MoMo." She plopped the baby in her crib and handed her a stuffed turtle.

The child squealed and rolled onto her back gazing at the toy with almost as much fascination as she'd given the tree.

"I think they're only in here," Heather said as she returned to Jonah.

He had a large plastic cup and was scooping the bugs up and throwing them outside into the winter's cold, his breath fogging under the outdoor light. "What are these things? They're creepy looking."

Grabbing another cup, Heather crept toward one of the lights. The skinny front bodies and bulbous rears of the insects streamed upward in a straight line, their triangular heads hovering over front appendages bent as if in prayer. "Oh my gosh. Jonah, they're praying mantis. I've never seen them so small."

This insect always gave her the willies with its big eyes and weird body. In high school, Mr. Parks, the biology teacher, showed them a video of the females devouring their mates during mating. The girls had gagged and giggled while the boys snorted at the ridiculous idea.

"Heather. Move. Don't just stand there." Jonah dumped another batch out the door.

As Jonah stomped back into the room, Heather crept toward the slow-moving line of infestation, extended her arm, and scooped up several, shrieking and jumping back when some fell to the floor.

"There must be a hundred of them," Jonah said dumping more out the front door. "Where did they come from?"

Heather shook her cup out the door. "I don't know. There must be an egg sac somewhere."

After several retrieval-and-dump sessions, a sick memory hit Heather. She edged closer to the Christmas tree and peered into the branches. A brown sac the size of an early pinecone hung from one of the cedar's limbs. A few of the insects dangled from the casing. "Remember that growth I told you about on the tree? The one you said was part of the branch? It must've been the egg sac." She shivered again. "I told you we should have bought a tree."

"No way I'm spending eighty dollars when there's a forest behind us," Jonah said, dumping another cup of insects out the door.

"Except you didn't get it from the forest, did you?" Heather couldn't hide the sharp note in her voice at that memory. She shook another cupful of bugs out the door.

At least, Jonah had the decency to look ashamed this time. "Yeah. I probably shouldn't have cut down one of Rory and Jewel's trees. I don't think they've noticed yet."

More bugs spilled from Heather's cup into the cold outdoors. "Seriously? Of course, they've noticed. It just hasn't occurred to them to look here. They probably expect some strangers stole their tree in the middle of the night. Not you, in broad daylight. I can't even invite them to our Christmas party, now."

"What's the matter? Can't handle it when you're not the one with the ax?"

She gasped at his accusation. He knew how much that mistake had cost her. How dare he? She turned her back and muttered under her breath, "Maybe the praying mantis has it right."

When Jonah had dragged the cedar tree home minutes after heading into the woods to "find a tree the way our forefathers did," she'd questioned the short time it took him to return. Anger over his lazy theft steamed her after he laughed and told her where he got it. Now, she fought the urge to toss the beautiful, infested tree and Jonah out the door.

The only thing keeping her from doing just that was the horrid memory of another cedar tree. One that changed her life forever. Was this nature's form of justice?

It had happened on a cold day like today, but in daylight, not long after school let out for the Christmas holidays. Her sister, Lexie, had that look about her. The one that said she was up to something. When the doorbell rang and Amber, Lexie's best friend, walked in wearing the same expression, Heather knew she needed to stop them from making a crazy mistake.

Most of the time, the three of them did stuff together, but that day neither girl invited her.

"Where are you going?" she'd asked as Lexie pushed past her, shoving her arms into her overcoat.

Heather grabbed her coat and followed them to the driveway. "Where are we going?"

Amber's hand hovered over the car's door handle. Lexie's did too. They shared a look over the top of the car that told Heather they wanted to be out of there fast, away from her suspicions.

Amber came up with the wildest schemes. Normally, Heather squashed them before her kid sister got into trouble. Today, it appeared she'd intervened just in time.

"We're running an errand for Amber's mom. That's all. Boring stuff." Lexie had turned and leaned against the car in a stance of nonchalance.

Warning bells rang in Heather's brain. They looked too calm, too cool to be telling the truth. Just moments ago, they'd rushed out of the house like two pups caught digging through the trashcan.

She wasn't stupid.

"I'm bored," she said. "I'll come with you."

Another glance flashed between the two conspirators. Amber shrugged. "Suit yourself."

Relieved, Heather climbed in the back seat of the blue Buick

Regal. "Where's your car?" Normally, Amber turned her nose up at her mother's ancient Buick.

Amber pulled out of the driveway. "Mom wanted me to take hers. The trunk has more room."

"Trunk? What are you picking up?"

The girls snorted.

Lexie turned her face away to look out the window. "Her mom wants a cedar tree for Christmas."

"I found the perfect one," Amber said.

The girls snorted, again.

"What's funny about that?' Heather eased forward trying to catch Amber's gaze in the rearview mirror.

"Remember, you asked to come," Amber said as she returned Heather's look.

Unease crawled up Heather's spine. "Why all the secrecy?"

Her sister twisted in the seat and gave her a grimace of a grin. "You'll see."

What was she missing? Heather flopped back in the seat, arms crossed. Unable to process schemes at Amber's lightning rates, she could only imagine. Giving up, she leaned forward, again. "Look you two. Whatever you've got planned, let me know before you get us all into trouble."

"Too late," Amber sang as she pulled into the Lakeside Park. "Either stay quiet or help us. You're not changing our minds."

"Why are you turning here?"

Neither girl answered. At a slow speed, Amber guided the car around the loop of the deserted parking area, Lexie leaning forward to search out the window. In summer, huge crowds enjoyed the park, but on a cold day in December, the place was deserted.

Heather followed Lexie's gaze, searching out the window, trying to guess what her sister was looking for.

She sighed in relief when Amber swung the car around the loop in the parking lot and started toward the exit. They were messing with her.

Then, Amber stopped the car beside three cedar trees lining the entrance to the park. The main road, a two-lane highway, ran a few hundred yards to their right. In plain view. Lexie and Amber hopped out of the car.

"You coming?" Lexie asked while Amber popped the trunk. She walked around the car, an ax in her hands.

They wouldn't, would they?

Heather jumped out of the car and rounded the rear in pursuit of Amber. "Are you crazy? This is park land. You could screw up your future. What about your scholarship?"

Running her hand along the ax's handle, Amber smiled. "Yours too...if we get caught." She pointed the head of the ax at Heather. "You're the lookout."

Not only did Amber have a tennis scholarship with State next year, but Heather had one for softball and academics. She needed both or else she'd never manage medical school. Cutting down the park's tree had to violate all sorts of ethics requirements. Not to mention the law.

Convinced they wouldn't go through with it, Heather turned back to the car.

Thwack!

She spun around. The cedar's branches shook from the lopsided blow.

Amber shoved the bottom limbs up, beckoning to Lexie. "Hold these branches out of my way."

Heather gulped at the raw scar on the tree's trunk and rushed around the car, swiping at her sister's willing hands. "She'll chop your hands off. Let go."

The ax swung again, a near miss of branches, Lexie, and most of the tree. Another small scar appeared in the bark to the left of the first one.

Heather crossed her arms. "You don't even know how to use an ax. Just stop."

Amber straightened and glared at Heather. "You might want to make sure we don't get company. Our futures are at stake, remember?" She wiped her nose on her sleeve, then repositioned herself. She took another swing.

As much as Heather hated to admit it, Amber was right. If they got caught, no one would ask whether she agreed to the plan or not. Lexie might tell the truth, but Amber wouldn't.

The sound of an approaching car on the highway sent ripples of terror down her spine. Heather ducked behind the car. "Get down."

The car drove by in a blur, never slowing.

Amber took another wild swing.

Sick resignation pooled in Heather's belly. The only way out of this was to finish and clear out before someone discovered them. She rounded the car, dodged another failed swing, then grabbed the ax.

Heather pointed it at Lexie. "You keep watch." She turned to Amber. "You'd think a tennis player would know how to swing an ax. Just stay back."

She swung.

The forest service had planted the trees over the summer, so the young tree's trunk wasn't thick yet. After a few more direct hits, it collapsed sideways with a loud crack, the branches rustling as they tumbled.

She hefted the ax over her shoulder. "Hurry up and get it in the car."

Relief washed over Heather in a wave of warmth that shifted to icy cold when a hiker emerged from the wooded area between them and the lake.

Good-bye scholarship. Hello community college.

She'd been the one holding the ax, so Heather got the worst of it. Lexie, at sixteen, got a slap on the wrist by the judge. Amber lost her scholarship, but her parents could afford State. She didn't suffer the same consequences as Heather. Or problems with her conscience, either.

Heather's guilt over that tree kept her from laying into Jonah about the one he stole from the neighbors. He knew, and his thoughtless betrayal hurt.

The tree did fill the trailer with a warm, Christmassy scent, and the colorful lights brightened up their dreary home. Made it cheerful. Almost.

At the door, she paused. They'd thrown most of the bugs into the yard. A few lay on the concrete step, their appendages waving a weak farewell to their short life. They'd killed them. Just like she'd killed that tree years ago. Just like Jonah killed the neighbor's tree.

Three praying mantes crawled around the bottom of the cup in her hand. She turned around and headed for the kitchen.

Mr. Parker, her high school biology teacher might welcome some new specimens for his lab. Maybe he'd forgive her for destroying his trust in her. She could still see the injured look in his eyes. Hear his words, "I thought you were smarter than that."

As for the cedars...

They'd gotten their revenge.

She stared out at the cold night, snow beginning to fall. A dish best served cold. Nature always won in the end, didn't it?

Just Me

"He never comes out." I stared at Tonya, a stupor of beer numbing my thoughts. We sat at a beat-up table in my apartment, papers and textbooks spread out, the detritus of a failed study session.

"I know." Tonya slapped at my arm in a clumsy attempt to comfort me. "Mary keeps him on a tight leash."

"He" was Cole, a chemistry student, tall, lean, with thick dark hair, and sea-green eyes that made me melt. Cole dated Mary Miles, Tonya's goody-goody sorority sister. I had never met Mary Miles, but I hated her.

"Did you drive by his apartment?"

I rolled my eyes at Tonya. "I see his car more than I see him."

Tonya started to laugh but cut it short when she caught my glare. She bit her lip and fought back the lingering smirk, her eyes growing distant for a few moments. Then she laughed anyway. "So, why don't you tell his car?"

"What?" I rubbed my face and tried to focus. How much *had* Tonya drunk?

"Tell his car how you feel."

I closed my eyes and tried to imagine this. Even drunk, I had my limits. Talking to a car at midnight went a bit too far.

"Look," Tonya leaned towards me. "Write a note and put it on the car."

Ooh! I could make sure I didn't say something stupid that way. I jumped up, knocking my chair over, and hauled my backpack up on the table. After rummaging for pen and paper, I plopped back down. "What should I say?" I stared at the crumpled paper ripped from a spiral notebook.

"What do you want to say?"

I shrugged. "I don't know."

"Ask why he doesn't come out on the weekends," Tonya said.

I chewed on the end of the pen for a moment. "I guess that'll work."

Dear Cole,

You never come out ~~at~~ on the weekend. Why? You need to come ~~party~~ have fun with us. ~~I can show~~ We could have a blast.

I read it aloud to Tonya.

"You know he's with Mary." Tonya's nose wrinkled in disgust.

A notion brightened my thoughts. Adding to the note, I read out loud, "Why don't you give someone besides M&M a chance?"

"M&M! That's great." Tonya's laughter brought tears to her eyes. "She really is an uptight little—"

"Should I sign it?" I studied the letter with drunken pride. I thought it sounded cool, but my courage only went so far. I couldn't bring myself to write Anna at the bottom.

Tonya re-read the letter. "M&M." She chuckled. "You don't want to sign it?"

I jiggled the pen between my fingers and stared at the TV. Johnny Carson leered at a scantily clad Bo Derek, Ed McMahon's bark of a laugh sounding in the background. Some women had it easy.

"What if he doesn't like it?" I wadded up the paper. "I'll see him every week in Dr. Jones' class."

"Wait." Tonya grabbed the paper from me, ripping the edge. "Sign it *Anonymous*." She tried to smooth the letter out.

"Anonymous?" I shoved my hair out of my face. "Nope. Don't like it."

"Look. Just write something. See how he reacts."

I thought about it. If I looked like Bo Derek this wouldn't be a problem. "See how he reacts first?"

Tonya handed me the pen.

"Then tell him it's just me?"

She bounced in her seat. "That's it! Sign it *Just Me*."

* * *

We rode in Tonya's old Ford, a huge tank of a car with rust on the hood. As she turned into the apartment complex, my heart leapt into my throat. On its heels rushed the aftermath of beer and pizza.

What if his car was there? What if his car wasn't there?

But there it sat, a light blue VW bug. Somehow it fit him.

"What if someone sees me?" My beer-hazed mind tried to contemplate the dangers of my actions.

"At this hour? Who cares? We're all drunk." Tonya nodded toward the car. "Do it."

I slunk down in the seat and peered out at the parking lot, twisting around to check it from all angles. Nothing moved. Inhaling like I was about to dive into the deep end, I shoved the heavy car door open, crouched down low, and scurried to the VW. Straightening enough to reach a wiper blade, I stuck the note underneath it and took a running dive back into Tonya's car.

She stepped on the gas, and we burst out laughing as the car's tires screeched out of there.

Exhilaration surged through me.

* * *

Saturday morning, I nursed a hangover and wondered whether Cole found the note. After hours of mood swings from panic, to exhilaration, to nausea, I drove by his apartment. The note was gone.

In class on Tuesday, I watched him out of the corner of my eye, obsessed over the thrill of our shared mystery. Looking for some sign he knew, I planned future letters from Just Me.

Since Cole parked in the same commuter lot as I did, I discovered I could tuck a note in his car door without breaking stride.

Sorry you had a cold over fall break. Take some Vitamin C.
Just Me

You should wear that green sweatshirt more often. You look hot in it.
Just Me

How did your mid-term project go? Heard you worked hard. Come out and celebrate!
Just Me

Next time try the butter pecan at the Dairy Bar. It's my favorite.
Just Me

Not once did we hear how he reacted to these letters. Cole's girlfriend, Mary, never mentioned them to Tonya. We hoped she didn't know.

Meanwhile, I reveled in my secret relationship with Cole, hoping for some chance encounter.

I ran into him at the library about a month later. We talked, but he didn't mention the letters. Probably didn't think we knew each other that well. Oh, if he only knew the familiarity I desired.

The semester wore on, but Tonya received no news. I got busy with finals, went on a few dates with a guy I met in English class, and gave up espionage for the real thing.

Until spring semester.

My biology lab partner, Beth, had just mentioned her chemistry class—Cole's major—and Just Me bounded to the forefront of my thoughts. Rested from her winter hibernation, she smiled and stretched.

I perched on the stool next to Beth, trying to locate a non-cooperative, single-celled invertebrate under the microscope. "Do you know Cole?"

"He's in my lab," Beth said.

I smiled. Maybe my luck was about to improve.

To encourage this thought, the pesky organism under the microscope swam into view and paused, centered on the slide. I took it as a sign.

Taking my gaze from the cellular blob, I looked Beth in the eye and smiled. "Want to have some fun?"

I knew she'd say yes. We hadn't known each other long, but I could tell Beth enjoyed excitement, especially if it made a boring lab interesting.

"Tell Cole that *Just Me* says hi."

It only took a few minutes to fill her in. Like little devils, we grinned at each other. In a way, I envied her access to Cole, but I'd settle for second-hand reports.

* * *

"You should have been there," Beth said in our next lab. "I said it while walking past him, and he spun completely around on his stool and grabbed my arm."

"He didn't."

She bobbed her head. "He kept asking, 'Who is it? Who is it?' But I didn't tell him."

The temptation to restart the letters seduced me. Even though I was dating someone, I succumbed. With Beth as my informant, Just Me returned.

Missed you at the soccer game. Just Me

Have you seen any movies? I love dark places. Come join me. Just Me

When are you going to relax and come out on Fridays? I like The Pub. Just Me

Beth managed to stuff the notes in Cole's books, his jacket pockets, and, as always, on his car. We giggled, plotted, and schemed all semester.

During the first week of finals, I handed her a new note hinting at my summer plans. She tilted her head to the side. "Another one this week? You're getting busy, aren't you?"

I shrugged. "You're leaving for the summer. I bet he is, too. This might be my last note until September."

The next day, I stopped studying long enough to run out for a burger. And ran into Cole.

"Hey, Anna. You eating here?"

"I had planned to get it to go," I said.

"Stay. Sit with me."

I looked toward the door, but his plea drew me. Who could deny those green eyes?

His first words spun my world upside down. "Did I ever tell you about the letters I kept getting?"

My stomach hardened into a ball. My mouth went dry. I grabbed for my soda and spilled it.

"Er, no. I need some napkins. Be right back."

What to do? Armed with napkins, I returned to the table, vowing to listen and say nothing. Mopping up the puddle, I asked, "What were you saying? Something about letters?"

"Yeah. This girl left me love letters." He shoved a handful of fries in his mouth.

I paused in wiping up my mess, soda dripping from the napkins. Left? What happened to the notes I gave Beth this week?

"Yeah." He pointed to the soaked napkins. "You might want to throw those away."

I hurried to the trash, fighting an unease that wouldn't let me breathe.

When I returned, he continued—where he found the letters, his efforts to figure out who wrote them, the things this person knew—and I listened.

I tried to act normal, but everything I murmured sounded phony. "Hmm ... Really ... Wow."

Then I asked *the* question, "So, any idea who it is?"

He smiled and stretched, bumping into my leg under the table. I jumped at the contact and slurped more drink.

"Oh, I know." Cole slid a fry through a puddle of ketchup and popped it in his mouth. He chewed with relish.

I held my breath, heart pounding.

"I thought it was this girl who lives in the same apartments as me, but," he lifted one shoulder, "it wasn't."

"You're sure?"

"Yep. I'm dating the mystery girl now."

What? Had Mary Miles taken credit for my hard work?

"Mary?" My voice squeaked up an octave. Just Me insisted I confess, but I swatted her aside.

"Nope. She found the letters and got mad. Didn't believe I didn't know who it was. We broke up."

I took a bite of burger and chewed over that information.

Had that been my plan? Drunk and besotted, had I really planned to break them up? My mind shied away from this turn of events and focused on the more critical. Who was impersonating Just Me?

"Sorry to hear that."

"Oh, it's all right. It was kind of fun figuring it out." Cole flashed another grin, his green eyes sparkling. "My friends are so jealous. Beth's beautiful."

I gagged on my burger and started coughing.

"You ok?" Concern crossed his face as he half-rose from his seat.

Grabbing a napkin, I waved him away, turned my back, and spat the half-chewed meat out. *Beth?* I rinsed my mouth with soda and swallowed, surprised at the pain swelling in my chest. "Did she tell you?"

Cole grinned. "Nope. Caught her in the act."

"Oh wow." I shoved my gullible ego down before it erupted with the truth.

"I should have been in class but forgot something. Caught her leaving it on my car." He laughed. "You should have seen her face. Adorable."

I swallowed my pain. "When?"

"About a month, I think." He screwed his face up in thought. "Yep. Four weeks tomorrow."

The smell of grease suffocated me. My stomach churned, a burp burning to escape. No wonder she questioned the extra letter the day before.

"So, where's your green sweatshirt?" I blurted out the one thing Beth never knew—my fascination with that shirt.

"It's a little warm for it now." He frowned. "Why do you ask?"

Good question. I scratched at a spot on the table.

"Anna?"

I took a deep breath and raised my eyes. "Just wondered."

"How do you know about the sweatshirt? I didn't mention it."

My voice rose just above a whisper. "I know."

Cole sat back, nodding. "Are you friends with her? Were you in on this?"

My rebellious head bobbed *yes*.

"You know what's weird? I wore that shirt on our first date. She ordered me to change it."

I promise I thought about it before I spoke. I did, but I hated how Beth benefitted from my letters and lied to me. Plus, he'd worn the sweatshirt and Beth didn't get it.

"She didn't say you looked cute? That your eyes look greener? That she wanted to run her hands up under it?"

Confusion creased Cole's brow.

I leaned forward, teeth bared. "That's because *she* didn't write the letters, Cole."

He blinked at me.

I wanted to shout but managed to keep my voice low. "Beth delivered them for me. She didn't write them. I did."

His reaction—back straight, clenched fists—made me go cold. I glanced at the door, positive I needed to go.

"I wore it all the time."

"What?" I stared at him, unsure if I'd heard correctly.

"After she, you … the letters. I wore that shirt all the time."

My heart bled a little.

His eyes looked like a scolded puppy's. "You stopped for a while."

"Stopped?" My mind struggled to keep up with his words.

"Leaving the letters."

"I'm dating someone," I said. "When I found out Beth knew you, I wrote a few more." I shrugged. "For fun."

"Yeah." He looked at me with renewed interest but then crossed his arms. "Mary found one of your notes. She threw it in my face."

Wait? I have to answer to his broken relationship while Beth gets to date him? I swept salt off of the table. "I'm sorry."

He leaned on his forearms. "I never expected you."

I didn't know whether to be insulted or proud. "So, what about Beth?"

He dropped back against the worn wood of the booth. "She lied, didn't she?"

I nodded. "To both of us."

The remains of our lunch lay spread over the table, greasy wax wrappings, balled-up napkins, my half-eaten burger. We both stared at it, but I don't think either of us saw it.

Cole raised his head until his gaze locked with mine. "I might be in love with her."

That wasn't what I wanted to hear. "Will you tell her?"

"Maybe. I don't know."

I wadded up my trash. Of course. Guys did stupid stuff all the time. Why should Cole be different?

I paused, my lunch remains balled up in my hands. "So, you never suspected me?"

"Nope."

"Why?"

He didn't reply.

Drained, disheartened, and not wanting to know his answer, I stood to leave. As I turned to walk away, he spoke again.

"You signed the first letter 'love.'"

I paused. "No, I didn't."

His nod was emphatic. "I wouldn't miss something like that. I still have the letters."

I thought back to the night it started and groaned. "I was drunk." I avoided his gaze. "I'm sorry."

I turned and hurried away. He didn't call me back this time.

I don't recall seeing much of Cole after that. I heard he broke up with Beth and started dating someone else soon after.

Sometimes, out of the blue, I think of Just Me, wondering what Cole is doing and if he still has the letters.

24

Maybe I'll find out next week at our thirty-year class reunion. I wonder what kind of car he drives now. Me? I bought an old, blue VW Beetle and restored it.

I love that car.

Pieces

I stare at my husband, my hand held to my temple.

He's yelling at me. The ringing in my ears blocks the sound. His voice comes to me muffled, like he's far away.

My head feels thick, heavy, jumbled.

He's still yelling. I see his red, angry face, his mouth roaring. I think I should care, but I don't know why.

The smell of scorching butter assaults me. I walk past him into the kitchen, where butter sizzles on the griddle, little puddles drying up, turning brown. I turn off the burner and stare at the nonstick surface.

"What are you doing?" Jimmy asks.

At least he's quit yelling. I hear him better, but my ears still muffle his voice. He looks at me differently. Curious. Maybe a little less mad.

"Why was this on?" I say.

He tilts his head and stares at me, blue eyes meant to pierce my soul. Somehow, it doesn't matter right now.

"You turned it on," he says and pinches his lower lip between his thumb and forefinger.

"Oh." I look away. Why did I turn it on? Raw cubed steak sits on a plate, a bowl of flour next to it.

"I must've been making dinner," I say. I don't remember doing it, but it's a cinch he wasn't cooking.

He crosses his arms, sarcasm drips from his voice. "You don't remember?"

I look back at him unsure of what to say. I grip the counter and hold on.

The baby's cries penetrate the shuttered walls of my ears. Angry screams from crying too long. I walk toward the nursery. She must be hungry.

"Where are you going?" Jimmy says, annoyance in his voice.

"I need to feed the baby."

He grabs my arm.

She's crying. She's hungry. Why would he stop me?

He drops his hand to his side. "You just fed her."

"I did?" I stumble back a step.

I don't remember feeding her or starting dinner. All I remember is the phone ringing. I had answered it. The rest is just a blank.

He's still staring at me, but his face registers ... fear. So that's what it looks like. Usually, I'm the one to show fear, and he loves putting it there. Why does he enjoy seeing *that* on my face?

"What's wrong with you?" He steps closer, concern radiates in his eyes.

I shake my head. Pain explodes in my brain, and a moan escapes.

Jimmy leads me to a chair. He hunkers down in front of me. "Are you ok?"

"I don't know."

"What did you do today?"

What did I do today? I don't know!

My hands start to shake.

He falls back on his heels, rubs his face. "What's your name?"

Relief. I know that. "Jill."

"Ok. Now, what did you do today?" His body leans toward me, begging for an answer.

I claw through my brain and come up empty. I search the room for clues. Check the clock—6:10. I glance at the TV—the news, President Carter.

What did I do today? I turn back to my husband, see the fear growing in his eyes.

"You took the baby to your Mom's." His voice sounds so gentle now.

I picture Mom's house, but not from today—not getting up, dressing the baby, driving the car.

She still cries. Jimmy tries to stop me, but I ignore him and go to the nursery, anxious for something normal. I pick her up, hold her close, and hum a lullaby, thankful I know the tune. Her cries settle into hiccuping as I carry her to the den and sit in the rocking chair.

She quiets to little snuffling sounds, her warm body cuddled against me in comfort. Whose? I bury my face in her baby scent.

Jimmy grabs the phone book. "What's your doctor's name?"

"What?"

"Your doctor?" He shakes his head at me. "You want me to call mine?"

I stare at the phone book willing it to give up its secrets, to tell me the name I need. I try to see it as it looks on the page. W – I – L.

"Wil ... Wil." A hazy image shapes in my mind. "Earl Willis," I say.

While Jimmy calls, I walk back into the kitchen. Something happened here. I stare back at Jimmy and remember the phone ringing, me answering it. *Then what?*

"The doctor said to bring you now," Jimmy says. "I'm calling Mom to baby-sit."

I nod once, flinching from a shooting pain, and turn back to my puzzle.

The phone call. A memory leaks in—from his boss. Was it important?

I had hung up and headed back to the kitchen when—

I shift the baby to my hip and stare at the small space. What happened here?

Jimmy stands by the phone, and my mind flashes to him looming over me and yelling, "What'd he say? What'd he say? What'd he say?" Leaving no room for me to answer, backing me into the dining room.

He's on the phone now with his mother. I listen to him try to talk, tears in his voice. "I don't know, Mom, she doesn't remember ... I don't know why ... no, yes. We'll be there soon."

I stand at the entrance to the dining room. Where was I when I forgot?

My gaze travels to those stupid overhanging cabinets. I return to that spot and stand in the same place. My fingers probe my temple. Tender, soft, pain.

I know what he did.

* * *

His mother comes out to the car and takes the baby.

"What's wrong, Jill?" Worry and confusion blink back from her eyes. I don't say anything. How can I? He's her son.

"She doesn't remember, Mama."

"Jimmy, what'd you do?" The scolding in her tone is obvious.

"Nothing, Mama."

He lies. I know it. She knows it. She looks at me, her mouth dropping open in that peculiar way it does when she suspects something but is afraid to speak of it. She breaks from my stare and looks down at the baby sleeping in her arms. I suspect she knows, probably has known, but she never says anything. No one saved her. Why would she save me?

We drive away.

In the car, Jimmy asks me, "Jill, who's Earl Willis?"

What game is he playing now? "I don't know. Why?"

"That's what you said your doctor's name is. It's not." He

takes his eyes off the road to penetrate me with his hard, blue gaze. "His name is Edmond Willis."

I shrug. Everything's jumbled.

Dr. Willis ushers me into an examining room. Jimmy follows close on my heels, not letting me out of his sight.

"So, tell me what happened," the doctor says.

Jimmy opens his mouth to speak.

Dr. Willis stops him. "I want her to tell me."

I look at him and pluck out the words. "I don't know. I was in the kitchen. I don't remember."

"Do you remember anything?"

I glance at Jimmy and swallow. He studies me like a bug.

"I've been trying. I know who I am. Where I am." I shrug. "I sort of remembered your name."

"What do you mean?"

"I told him Earl Willis."

The doctor pauses and thinks for a moment. "Do you know an Earl?"

I claw through my brain, searching for clues. Dr. Willis waits, watching me.

Earl...Earl?...Earl Willis... It hits me. "Earl Wilson! My parent's minister."

The doctor nods. "Easy to confuse. Both familiar names. Tell me about today."

"Jimmy says I went to Mom's today. I don't remember ... I only remember that the phone rang."

Jimmy's head jerks up. I hadn't told him I remembered that.

My heart hammers, and I look away, seeking refuge in the doctor's kind face. "I answered it. I don't remember anything else."

"Did you fall? Hit your head?" Dr. Willis asks.

"My ears were ringing. Everything was muffled." I stop and listen for a moment. "It hurts to shake my head."

Doctor Willis lifts my chin and flashes a light in each of my eyes. He probes my head.

"Ouch." I shrink back, tender pain swelling in my temple.

"Here?" His hands apply pressure.

"Yes."

Dr. Willis examines my scalp. "It looks a little inflamed. Did you hit your head?"

"I don't know."

He turns to Jimmy. "Did she?"

Jimmy shakes his head. He drops his face into his hands. "She wouldn't tell me what he said on the phone. She hung up and walked away. I followed her, and..." He starts to cry, his shoulders shaking.

I can't believe it. He almost admitted it. I say nothing and wait.

Doctor Willis' gaze shifts back and forth between us. He's propped against the counter covered with all of his doctor stuff: jars of tongue depressors, cotton balls, stainless steel instruments. He picks up the reflex hammer and bounces it in his palm. Maybe he'll whack Jimmy with it. *Wouldn't that be wonderful?!*

The doctor comes back over to me and tilts my head up, searching my face. There's a question in his eyes I can't answer. He shines the pinpoint light into my pupils again and flicks it away several times. His fingers probe my scalp, withdrawing when I flinch.

He turns to Jimmy. "Were you yelling at her?"

Jimmy nods.

Dr. Willis crosses his arms and studies the floor. After a few moments, he looks at me again, that same unanswered question reflected in his wrinkled brow. "It's obvious you hit your head, *somehow.*"

I stare back, unable to answer him.

He uncrosses his arms and turns to Jimmy. "But she doesn't have a concussion."

Jimmy looks hopeful.

"Sometimes, under stress, we can have small nervous breakdowns," Dr Willis says. "That could be what happened. Why she lost some of her memory. We call it short-term amnesia."

Jimmy puts on his serious, we're talking man-to-man face. He nods.

The doctor's going to let Jimmy off the hook? Why doesn't he help me? I glance at Jimmy. He's beyond remorse. He's found his out. I lost mine.

I think of my baby sleeping in his mother's arms. I have to go back. My moment of help vanished as quickly as it appeared. I refuse to cry.

"Will I ever remember?" I whisper.

Dr. Willis tilts his head to the side. "I don't know. You might, but don't count on it." He stands over Jimmy. "You may never know what that phone call was about."

We walk out of the examining room.

Dr. Willis escorts us to the door. "No charge for this one. Just take it easy tonight. Let me know if things get worse."

Jimmy shakes the doctor's hand, and we walk away. I wonder how he'll use a nervous breakdown against me in the future.

He drapes his arm over my shoulder. I cringe inside, but I let him.

John-E-Mail

~∞~

To: John@freedommail.com
From: Sweetiepie321@girlmail.com
Date: February 15, 2006, 2:13:32 am
Subject: Happy Valentine's Day

Dear Johnny,

I missssss you so much. I thought today would be awful! All of the girls getting flowers and candy and stuff. Depressed me! But then I thought about you defending our country. Boy did I fell guilty. I'm so selfish. : (

Did you get the card and candy, yet? I hope I sent them in time.

I felt so left out, today. I rented Cold Mountain because Nicole Kidman knows how I feel. You know how she writes her boyfriend and tells him to come home to her and he does? I wish you could do that. I was going to veg out and watch it all alone.

. . .

But, anyway, Trip and Julie made me go to some crazy party with them. I'm soooooo glad that they did cause I met a guy who just got back from Iraq. He made me feel so close to you. He told me stories and stuff that I know you can't. I wish it was you telling me these things. Come home to me.

Lots of love and hugs,
    Ally

To: Sweetiepie321@girlmail.com
From: John@freedommail.com
Date: February 15, 2:12:54 am
Subject: Valentine

Hey baby! Happy Valentine's Day! I wanted to call you tonight, but I couldn't get through. We've had busy days. Lots happening. I thought about you today when we passed a girl by the side of the road. We thought she was just watching the trucks, but it got crazy and that's the last time I had time to think til now. I miss you. Wish I could have talked to you today.

Love ya! Johnny

To: John@freedommail.com
From: TheTrip@myemail.com
Date: February 15, 2006, 3:03:24 pm
Subject: Sorry Dude

Hey!

Sorry guy my cell died. I had your ring and was going to give Ally the phone when you called. I failed you man. She was really down when we picked her up. I know she'll say yes. The party helped, though. She kept talking about you to some marine from Iraq.

To: TheTrip@myemail.com
From: John@freedommail.com
Date: February 15, 2006, 12:43:19 pm
Subject: Re: Sorry Dude

No problem about the phone. I'll work on another time to propose. They say I'll be home in June. Maybe I'll wait until then.

Who's the marine?

To: John@freedommail.com
From: Sweetiepie321@girlmail.com
Date: February 15, 2006, 7:16:43 pm
Subject: Miss You

Dear Johnny,

. . .

Did you notice that we were emailing each other at the same time! Wow, we are so meant to be! I got your card. It would've been better if you were here, though. I miss you so much. I saw Glen, again. The marine. He keeps telling me about his adventures in Iraq. It sounds so dangerous. I had a nightmare about you last night. You were in trouble and Glen saved you! Isn't that funny? It felt so real. Please, please, please be careful.

Gotta go. Glen is taking me over to Julie's house. He makes me feel so close to you.

Love ya!

To: TheTrip@myemail.com
From: John@freedommail.com
Date: February 16, 2006 9:16:44 am
Subject: Glen

Trip! Who's this Glen guy? What's going on?

To: John@freedommail.com
From: Sweetiepie321@girlmail.com
Date: February 17, 2006 2:23:21 am
Subject: I feel stupid

Dear Johnny,

. . .

You must think I'm a ditz! Glen told me that if you were emailing me at 2 am in Iraq that it's not 2 am here. I thought it was SO romantic how we emailed each other at the same time and I was just wrong. How stupid can I be? Please don't think I'm dumb.

I miss you. Glen's stories make your world so real to me. Do you know he was Special Ops? Isn't that exciting?

Ally

To: John@freedommail.com
From: TheTrip@myemail.com
Date: February 17, 2006, 6:14:14 pm
Subject: Re: Glen

Dude, Glen's bad news. I met Julie and Ally for lunch and he was there. All the girls love him. He's so full of it. He claims he captured Saddam. What crap! They're all eating it up, especially Ally. She keeps saying it makes her closer to you but man I think she's getting pretty close to old Glen > : {

Better watch out!

To: John@freedommail.com
From: MarineforLife@hero.com
Date: February 17, 2006 11:56:33 pm
Subject: Ally

John,

Hey man, you don't know me, but we're brothers. I got back from Iraq last month and I met Ally a few days ago. You're one lucky dude. I lost my girl while I was over there, so I'm gonna keep a close eye on Ally for you. Don't worry man. I got ya covered.

Glen

To: John@freedommail.com
From: Sweetiepie321@girlmail.com
Date: February 18, 2006 6:14:59 pm
Subject: You!

Hi Johnny!

You know how you always beg me to get out more? Well, I'm doing it! Glen is making sure of it. He says he's keeping the guys away for you. Isn't that sweet? Did he email you? I gave him your address so he could encourage you too. He's done so much over there. He helps me so much. I don't miss you as much when he's around.

Ally

To: Sweetiepie321@girlmail.com
From: John@freedommail.com
Date: February 20, 2006, 11:47 pm
Subject: Re: You!

Dear Ally,

I love you. I miss you. I'm a little worried about this Glen guy. What unit is he from? Be careful baby? I can't wait to see you. I have a big surprise for you.

Love John

To: Sweetiepie321@girlmail.com
From: John@freedommail.com
Date: February 21, 2006, 11:21:26 pm
Subject: Checking In

Ally,

What's up? I've not heard from you in days. I miss you. I think about you all the time. They're sending us home in May, now. I know it keeps changing, but I can't wait to see you. I've got something big to talk to you about.

Love John

To: Sweetiepie321@girlmail.com
From: John@freedommail.com
Date: February 22, 2006, 10:17:43 am
Subject: Are you OK?

Hey baby, what's up? I miss you. I love you. Is your email not working? I miss getting your daily emails. Waiting for you.

John

To: John@freedommail.com
From: Sweetiepie321@girlmail.com
Date: February 23, 2006, 4:39:12 am
Subject: Re: Are you OK?

Dear John

The Wall

The evening sun slanted across the rolling lands and glinted off the river snaking like a silver jewel in the distance. The brilliant oranges and yellows of flowers faded in the dusk, lost in the scraggly greenish-brown underbrush. How many nights had Marcus stood, enthralled by nature's canvas of color? He hated to change it, but other beauty might disappear from his life if they didn't create the barrier and protect their lands.

"I don't see why you want this wall." Serena, his wife, squinted at Marcus.

She'd crept up on him like one of the snakes slithering in the underbrush, a frown creasing her forehead, turning her older and less attractive in his eyes. He knew this expression of hers. Had always hated when she turned it on him. At least she wasn't dressed in power reds today. That red wardrobe always announced the onslaught of a battle, verbal, of course, and difficult to navigate, just like some of the terrain beyond the border.

"I'm not the only one who wants it." He walked away from her, toward the edge of the property, hearing her sigh, then her footsteps rustled in the grass behind him. Her shadow stretched out before her, arriving first, like a looming demon waiting to strike.

Arms crossed, she stared toward the border. "I don't get it. What's the big deal? So, a few cross over. Seriously, I don't see the problem."

How many times had they discussed this? It felt like an infinity, as their grandson would say. "It will protect us and our land. Keep it private and safe."

"Safe?" She spun toward him, hands on her hips. "From what? They mean no harm. Just trying to find joy in life. We've lived here thirty years. Why worry about it now?"

Don't look at her, he thought. At the meeting the other day, they advised everyone not to engage dissenters anymore. It worked. At least, that's what Jeff and Milly and Trenton had claimed. Why get dragged through the dirt with someone who refused to listen or understand?

He tried to tell the others that silence wouldn't keep Serena quiet. His wife carried on full conversations with him all the time, and him not adding a single word.

But this wall had changed the conversations, forced the two of them to opposite sides.

"A wall will destroy this landscape. Make it tacky, ugly. I don't want to sit on the porch every day staring at a monstrosity."

Silence again.

She was right. That's why he came out here each night and every morning. To store up the memory.

They needed the wall, though. Their lands were getting torn up. Just last week, he'd found some of the fruit trees knocked down, and her golden lantana ruined. Nothing could salvage them. Something had ripped into the beautiful flowers like a thief tearing through a room looking for treasure. So, he'd shown her the destruction, his heart aching for the tears welling in her eyes. Her mother planted that lantana and the pear trees. They had survived decades until now.

"And it's so expensive." Her one-ended dialogue continued. "They should spend it on something worthwhile instead. Not this. Money is supposed to add value, Marcus, not destroy beauty."

"The wall will add value." The moment he spoke the words, he wanted to kick himself. *Don't speak, that's the key.* Yet, she always drew him into her conversation like a huge magnet.

He waited for her counterargument, but it didn't come. Had she walked away? He slid his eyes to the side, checking that she still stood there. She did, her head tilted to the sky; her features softened into the sweet innocence he fell in love with ages ago. In the dwindling light, something glittered on her cheek. A tear? If she cried, what would he do? It tore at his soul when she revealed her true nature hidden behind the constant barrage of words. Her own wall of protection.

Always able to sense his attention, Serena glanced his way then pointed up. "Look, the first star," she whispered. "I wish I may, I wish I might, have the wish I wish tonight."

Against the royal blue of the darkening sky, the single light twinkled. "Like a diamond in the sky," he whispered back, unable to fight their age-old tradition.

Silence, sweet quiet stood between them. What did she wish for? He didn't need to ask. She always told her wish, unaffected by the admonition to keep it secret until the world turned on its axis and granted her desire. And tonight? Every wish she'd shared with him followed the trail of her thoughts moments before the request. Not that he believed in star wishes, but if you were going to wish, why not take a moment and choose something strong, valuable? He never understood her willingness to go with the flow, to wish upon a star, believe in it, and still not abide by the rules.

"Know what I wished for?" The smile he loved resonated in her voice.

He snorted in amusement. "No wall?"

"Nope."

* * *

43

Serena fought back the grin she wanted to flash at Marcus' obvious shock from her denial. Heavens, she loved him. But his unbendable nature—that unwillingness to look at things from a different angle and consider others—made her want to rap him on the head sometimes. See if it echoed like the Tin Man in *The Wizard of Oz*. Except, Marcus did have a heart. It peeked out when she least expected it, like the rabbits she occasionally saw in the underbrush, a head popping up in surprise at her approach. Dashing off before the danger of discovery.

His tone rang with disbelief, edging into sarcasm. "You didn't wish for the wall?"

It rankled her nerves a bit, that tone. "Nope." And then she couldn't help but put her hands on her hips and toss back her displeasure. "And why would I lie to you about that? It's not like I keep things from you."

An interminable silence passed while she watched him chew on her words, or maybe his. She never knew what he thought before he spoke.

"I give," Marcus said, turning to face her. "What did you wish for?"

"I wished that you would remember how much you cherish this landscape."

His eyes widened in surprise.

"Don't you see," she sidled up next to him, tucking her arm in his. "This is our homeland, our heritage. How can we close ourselves off and proclaim to everyone, 'Keep Out'?"

"To protect it," he said. "I'm tired of the trucks and four-wheelers tearing up the ground. Not to mention fighting off the wild animals that wander into our lands."

"What if they knock it down? They could tunnel under or climb over."

"Maybe." He pulled away from her. "If you'd quit encouraging the neighborhood kids to run through here, it wouldn't be a problem. They see it as their extended playground. Then they grow up and learn how to drive."

"I don't encourage them. You discourage them."

"Same difference," he said. "What's done is done. The HOA is coming tomorrow to finalize the paperwork."

She sighed and looked to her left and right, noting the lights coming on in the houses down their street. Her parents bought the house in the cul-de-sac to secure this view. She and Marcus bought it from them when they moved into a retirement home. The land behind was protected, part of national lands. No one had ever ruined the view of the mountains and river in the distance. Until now.

"Can't we at least make it a picket fence? Something pretty?"

Marcus pinned her with his piercing blue eyes, the ones that caught her heart and held it as a willing lover for the last three decades. Lately, that relationship struggled to survive. Why couldn't he see the destruction building between them?

His chest rose and fell in the way she knew indicated he was planning his next words. Would he speak them or decide to be silent again? Which did she want him to do?

He spoke. "It was going to be a surprise, but we decided to do something decorative instead. Aluminum posts. They look like wrought iron and will be spaced close enough together to keep out the larger animals."

Glee like she'd felt when he first asked her on a date rose in her soul. Maybe he did see the damage to their lives. Maybe he did hear her.

Serena threw her arms around him. "The rabbits can still get in? And I'll still see the river?"

His smile looked a bit sheepish as he nodded. "You'll still have your view, darlin'. I promise."

"You know what that means?" A sly grin traced her lips.

"What?" He gazed down at her.

"I got my wish."

He breathed a short chuckle and pulled her closer. "You always do, Serena. You always do."

The Devil's Wife

"Have you ever heard the superstition about it raining while the sun's shining?" The young woman half-peered up at the counselor, half-not, her gaze returning to the worn spot she traced on the chair's armrest.

"I think so." Isaac watched her finger circle over and over on the spot on his chair.

Shifting her gaze to the painting on the wall, a distant look in her eyes, she said, "You know. The one about the devil beating his wife." She paused, then looked up at Isaac. "I always hated that one." Cocking her head to the side, a grimace of a smile crossed her face.

"Do you believe in superstitions?" Isaac asked.

"Oh no, not really." She laughed. "I even had a solid black cat once. Those were probably the luckiest days of my life. Ya know? Before I met Dan."

"Was meeting Dan unlucky?"

"Huh. Some question that is," she said. "I wouldn't be here now if I'd never met him."

For a moment, the woman crossed her arms and slid down in the chair, folding in on herself.

Isaac shook his head. Every time Dan's name came up she took this posture. Often, it indicated the end of the session, or the productive part, at least. He tried to shift her back to safer territory. "So, what about rain when the sun's shining? What does that mean?"

"Oh that." She sat straighter and rubbed more fabric away on the arm of the chair.

Silence. Isaac waited several minutes, but she never looked up, her finger speeding up as it ran around and around the spot.

"I believe it goes like this," Isaac said. "If it's raining when the sun is shining, then the devil's beating his wife. Right?"

"That's the one." She switched to her thumb rubbing away the fabric.

A new spot would appear on the chair if he reupholstered it, but it might be time.

As if reading his mind, the woman looked up. "I guess everyone rubs this spot, huh?"

"I guess so."

"We're all just a bunch of nervous nobodies, aren't we?" She caught her right hand in her left, gripping so hard the knuckles turned white.

"I wouldn't say that." Isaac looked into her eyes. They were a lovely shade of blue, like the ocean in some exotic vacation spot. "Do you think you're a nobody?"

"Dan said I was."

"I see."

"Not that Dan knows anything. I just heard it enough. Until I, you know, started believing it." Her hand escaped the claw of the left one and circled the spot again.

"Do you still believe it?" He forced himself to stay relaxed and not lean forward while he waited for her answer. She always got stuck when it came to stepping over the precipice of denying Dan's words.

"Not always, but sometimes. Like when I did it."

"Did what?" Isaac stiffened in the shoulders but forced his face to remain neutral.

"What we've been talking about, of course."

She now fidgeted with the locket on her necklace, sliding it back and forth on the short gold chain. If Isaac listened hard enough, he could hear the rasp of it as metal rubbed against metal.

"Why don't you tell me about it?"

The wariness in her gaze gave Isaac pause. He knew the calculated look, the searching for a decision, trying to determine whether to share or not. What confession might spill out in his office today? He hoped it wasn't one the law required him to report.

Her shoulders slumped, and she dropped the necklace. "I feel really foolish about it. I was so horrified afterward. What if someone had seen me?"

"Nobody saw?"

"I don't think so. Least, I hope not."

Isaac waited.

"Well, you know what you're supposed to do, don't you?" She turned her head to the right a bit, a sideways glance in his direction rather than straight on.

"I'm not sure that I do," Isaac said, unsure what her question referred to. Hide a body?

"Well, it was right after Dan had ... well, you know. I was pretty badly bruised. I'd had enough."

She paused for a minute, examining her thumbnail.

Suddenly, the woman looked him square in the eye. "So I did it." Her voice reverberated around the room. "They say you're supposed to stick a knife in the ground at the foot of a tree. That's supposed to stop the devil."

"From beating his wife?"

"Yes." She scooted forward, sitting on the edge of the chair. "So I grabbed my butcher knife and ran out in the pouring rain with that sun shining down on me. And do you know what?"

"What?"

Eyes bugging out, she leaned toward him. "No sooner did I drive that knife into the ground than the sun scuttled behind the clouds."

She leaned back, a self-satisfied smile on her face.

Gentle Snow

The world lay quiet and still under a fresh blanket of white. Sarah glided between the trees, reveling in the perfect silence interrupted only by the swish of her cross-country skis and the occasional creak of a branch settling under its frosted dressing. At the edge of the wood, she paused, peering at the quiet house in the clearing. Behind her, through the woods, her truck waited, loaded for her long-anticipated vacation.

The house loomed stark in the snow, its monstrosity amusing and sickening her. Her gloved fingers caressed the scar above her right eyebrow, a remnant of Eric's last violent outburst six years ago. While he slept, drained by his drunken rage, she'd packed up Gloria and moved to this obscure Colorado town, hoping he'd never find them. Five years to the day, Eric showed up in the local hospital's ER, smiling his most charming smile. Stomach churning at the sight, Sarah pushed another nurse in his direction.

Instead, he followed her, with his heavy boot clomps, and leaned against the institutional-white wall, a smug grin on his face. "You can't get rid of me that easily."

"Oh, but I did," Sarah said, her voice low to avoid co-worker eavesdropping. "We're no longer married."

"Yes, but we will be neighbors. Walking distance. The house behind yours. I'll know everything you do."

The hairs stood up on her neck. Eric had not only found them. He shared a property line.

She had nothing to hide, but she knew he excelled in creating something from nothing. She fit in this town. Would Eric ruin it for her? For their daughter? Just to exert some control?

From the vantage point of the tree line, Sarah made a thorough study of Eric's property, checking for signs of life. Their daughter, Gloria, now twenty years old, said he planned to leave early this morning on his own vacation. She couldn't help but wonder if Eric's trip might be a ploy to follow her out of town.

The strained phone call last night agitated her.

"Gloria," Sarah had said. "I can't find my blue ski jacket. Did you borrow it?"

"Um, yeah, I guess I did," Gloria's distracted voice floated across the airwaves.

Sarah relaxed at her daughter's confirmation. "I need it back. The directions to the cabin are in the pocket."

"Uh oh. Um, Mom?" Gloria's voice already apologized. "I left it at Dad's house."

Sarah shoved the memory of the disturbing phone call to the walled-off corner of her mind reserved for Eric issues. It jabbered back at her: if Gloria hadn't borrowed the jacket, she wouldn't be in this mess.

Sarah squared her shoulders, satisfied that Eric had already left, and slid out into the open. She hoped to be in and out in minutes.

The bunny statue on the back porch hid the key. Eric's habits never changed.

Sarah leaned her skis against the wall, brushed the snow from her coat, and pulled off her boots. Dry socks wouldn't track any snow into the house to puddle and dry into a dingy spot waiting for discovery. She gripped the house key in her leather-gloved hands. It slid into the lock and, with a click, she entered the laundry room. Sarah and Gloria had explored the large house during its construction, long before she knew it would become his lair. The question was whether Eric had found the jacket.

On tiptoe, Sarah crossed the laundry room and entered the kitchen. She blinked at the stark whiteness of it all. Gloria had told her everything was white, but the reality gave her pause. Outside, snow fell steadily, beautiful in its pure form. Indoors, the color appeared unnatural, like the hospital.

"Never changes," Sarah said and headed for the great room and the coat closet beyond there.

A coffee cup sat on the kitchen counter. Sarah froze.

Nothing moved in the house. The carriage clock on the mantle ticked, ticked, ticked, echoing in the empty house. Sarah waited a full two minutes, heart pounding rhythm with the clock. Silence.

She approached the cup as if it were a snake. A full cup. The burnt aroma of over-brewed coffee swelled in her nostrils. On the counter beside the stove, a coffee-maker announced the time, 9:34 a.m., above a half-full pot. The red burner light winked at Sarah. Eric's fastidiousness would never allow him to leave the kitchen dirty. And, by his definition, this was dirty.

Confused, Sarah balanced on her toes and stretched a palsied hand toward the cup, the nurse's finesse gone from her fingers. It held no warmth. She snatched her hand back and held her breath, counting the seconds. Pungent sweat, rank with fear, rose from the layers of protective winter clothing, clouding her senses. Silence stretched around her, blanketed by the still-falling snow.

Sarah teetered on the edge of uncertainty.She inched across the room and opened the door to the garage. Eric's SUV, gleaming and loaded to go, glared at her.

She scurried a panicked retreat to the back door. Outside, she shoved feet into boots, strapped on skis, and hastened away from the porch.

A flurry of wings to her left froze Sarah in her tracks. Several birds hopped and pecked around the feeders, a bag of birdseed half-buried in the snow, little bits and pellets scattered around it. Beside the feast, almost covered by the heavy snow, lay a large shape.

Unstrapping the skis, Sarah lunged through the drifts, cursing the birds. They squawked and banked up into the sky, a dazzle of wings and darkness against the light.

"Eric?" Sarah shoved the snow away from his shape, cringing at the pink slush beneath his face. A gash across his forehead seeped a small amount of blood, the flow congealing in the below-freezing temperature. Rust-red stained the edge of the concrete bird bath beside her.

The nurse took over, yanking off gloves and checking for a pulse. Nothing. She tore open the parka, leaning her ear against his chest. His body felt like ice, the blood withdrawing from the external limbs to maintain inner warmth. *Was he alive?*

"Eric!" Sarah said, her sharp angry tone echoing in the snow-muffled air. Returning birds squawked and flew away. She laid her fingers under his nose, but the cold air froze the feeling from her hand.

Boots crunching across the yard, Sarah grabbed the key and shoved the laundry room door open again. She raced into the kitchen and grabbed for the phone. She'd never make her train now. Every time she tried to enjoy life, Eric interfered, even now, without planning to.

Sarah pressed nine.

She pressed one.

Index finger hovering over the final digit, Sarah hesitated. She would miss her train. Eric had won again. Reluctant eyes scanned across the starkly clean room and out the window where the birds clustered around the seed again. *Was* he alive?

* * *

The white marble counter felt cool against Sarah's arms as she leaned over and picked up the reheated cup of coffee. She sipped.

The floor-to-ceiling windows provided a panoramic view of the long, sloping yard that ended at the stand of trees, now frosted in white. The tracks from her cross-country skis had disappeared some time ago.

Her gaze drifted to the ground near the bird feeders. His body was almost covered again, the blood-pinkened snow hidden under the heavy snowfall. Just a small piece of his parka peeped out at the world. Soon, no one would guess his body lay there. It was perfect. Expected to accumulate three feet overnight, the snow would hide him until the thaw.

Sarah finished the cup of coffee and placed it in the dishwasher. True to expectations, a heavily rinsed load of used dishes waited, the lemon-scented liquid detergent already squeezed into its designated cup inside the door. She pressed the normal wash cycle.

The body was no longer visible. If she was right, he had not made reservations for his trip. That one habit caused many fights during their marriage. Eric always argued he could get a better deal by negotiating face-to-face with a desk clerk. Of course, there had to be a vacancy in order to do that.

With Eric's body covered and enough accumulation to hide the suspicious mound, Sarah felt safe leaving. She always did what was expected of her, but not today. Odds were, he was long dead before she arrived. The cold coffee and his early departure plans agreed with that assumption. His body would not rot, entombed in the snow until someone missed him. Even then, the snow might hide him during the search.

She retrieved her coat and left everything the way he would. The key slid back underneath the stone bunny, and she slipped her feet back into the boots and strapped on her skis. By the time anyone thought to look for him, her tracks would have disappeared, too.

At the bird feeder she paused, recalling the image of Eric's body under the snow, then turned her back and headed down the hill into the woods, a smile creasing her face. No other home was in sight. Eric moved so close to upset her—funny how that had turned out.

Skis packed into the truck, Sarah stopped only to answer the vibration of her cell phone.

"Hello?"

"Mom. Hey. Have you left yet?"

"Gloria! Yep. About an hour ago. What's up?"

"Nothing. Just wanted to tell you to have fun."

Sarah smiled as she sat in the driver's seat. "Oh, I will. Love ya, hon."

Snow swished off the windshield as the wipers went into action, the only other sound the crunch of snow under her tires. Sarah drove down the mountain, a giddiness gathering in her chest. A giggle escaped her lips, then another. Soon, she laughed with abandon.

She never saw the patch of ice.

The wipers continued, squeaking back and forth against the cracked windshield while falling snow blanketed the underside of her overturned truck.

Books, Brandys, and Blue-Hairs

I hated it when my lunch hour ended in the middle of something big. Now I'd have to wait until tomorrow to see who tampered with the brakes. Resigned to my fate, I reshelved *Little White Lies* among Jennifer Lynn Barnes' other titles on the bookstore's shelves. Two copies remained alongside single copies of her most recent novels.

I don't like to read books unless they have several on the shelf. I made that mistake when reading *A Feast for Crows*. I should have known better with the popularity of the *Game of Thrones* TV adaptation. Before I could finish the book, the copies dwindled down to one, and then none.

After that, I started reading older books, not the ones on the best seller list.

As I turned from the shelf, Reggie, a salesclerk, stopped me. "Gail, do you know who wrote *Lost Lake*?" A middle-aged woman hovered behind him. "She also wrote something about sugar?"

I smiled in appreciation. "I think you mean Sarah Addison Allen. She wrote *The Sugar Queen*. You'll find her in general fiction."

"Thanks."

I nodded and gathered my things to leave. A man in a dress shirt and tie stared at me as I stepped into the center aisle. The new manager. He'd been watching me all week.

It might be time to buy something again.

The clearance table offered inconspicuous books that I sometimes bought and later donated to Meals on Wheels. That was the best I could do for now. A clutter-free workplace and my Dad's abhorrence of books made it difficult to keep—much less read—any books. I perused the markdowns for a cheap selection.

The bright yellow covers of a large stack of *Financial Planning for Dummies* caught my attention. I doubted the title's rude lure could solve my financial troubles. Not unless it hid a treasure map between the pages. I needed guidance on how to move out of my parents' house for the second time in my adult life, not a financial self-help book unable to sell at a reduced price.

My gaze landed on a paperback copy of *The Secret Garden*. On clearance? I picked it up and thumbed through the pages, pausing at familiar images of Mary and Colin.

I'm ten years old again, tears streaming down my face as Dad storms through the house tossing books into the roaring fireplace.

Mom tries to stop him, but he ignores her, bent on destruction. "Books killed him, Doris. There's no two ways about it."

Dad's brother, Joe, had loved books, especially how-to ones. He believed he could do anything explained in a book. *Foraging for Mushrooms* was the last book he read. Dad's book-destroying tirade erupted two days after the funeral.

The only book Mom managed to save that day was the Bible. "Oh no you don't, Wade." She yanked the blessed book out of his hand. "Not God's Word."

Like a balloon pricked with a needle, my father's shoulders had drooped under the weight of his grief. He broke down, crying in large, terrifying sobs.

Unnerved by the memory, I put the book back and left the store. Bright sunlight blinded me for a moment, but I'd made this trek almost every day for six months. I could walk it with my eyes closed as long as no one ran over me. The book store's proximity to George's Salon was one of two benefits of my miserable job. The other? A paycheck.

I entered the salon through the back door. A quick glance in the waiting area told me my next appointment, Margaret Reuters, had arrived. Two women, seated on either side of her, chatted, feet tapping in some unknown urgency. Margaret glanced back and forth, an obvious eavesdropper to their conversation. I chuckled as they made annoyed eyes at her but continued talking.

George, stick thin and pompous, sauntered up to me. He smiled at the ladies, took me by the arm, and steered me away. Between gritted teeth, he said, "Get that blue hair out of my waiting room."

George hated my mom's old customers. Called them busy body blue-hairs even though none of their hair had the distinctive hue of the generation before them.

I escorted Margaret to my tiny booth. The empty shelves, my quiet protest against George's rules about clutter, held one small and dusty fake fern Mom had given me.

"How's Boxer?" I asked as I shampooed Margaret's short gray hair.

A chuckle escaped her wrinkled mouth. "That mangy cat! I ought to put him to sleep."

I smiled. Nothing changed between Margaret and that cat. He was blind, partially lame, and beyond ugly, but she adored him. "What'd he do now?"

"He's marking again. All over my dining room."

"Marking? Isn't he like forty years old?"

She angled her gaze at me in exasperation. "Eighteen and you know it."

I nodded and turned her to face the mirror. "So, are we going blonde today?"

"Oh yes." She preened. "For the cabana party."

We laughed at our running joke. Margaret Reuters, at eighty-six, was definitely not going blonde.

I snipped her bob back into shape and smiled at the transformation this simple cut gave her.

She started coming to me a few months after Mom closed her shop. Like most of Mom's clients, she wanted a weekly wash and set. After a month, I convinced her to save time and money and let me bob it. Now I saw her every five weeks instead of one. She draws the line at blonde hair.

My next customer belonged to the wine-and-cheese set. George, the salon owner, kept scheduling these ladies with me, but it never worked out.

With their turned-up nose jobs, I feared they'd drown during their shampoo, or the cuttings might settle in their nostrils and make them sneeze. What do you say to a woman whose jewelry would pay rent on a nice apartment for a year or more?

I studied the newest nominee for my clientele—petite, brunette, hairstyle a replica of the latest trendy style. Diamonds dangled from her ears before she unfastened them and dropped them into my hand for safe keeping. Thick, gold bracelets jangled on her wrists and a delicate gold chain draped around her neck, a solitaire diamond suspended from it.

I could live quite comfortably on the sale of those jewels. I doubted she had a mangy cat, either—probably some Persian left at the groomer while "Mummy" got pampered.

"What do you want to do today?" I fluffed my fingers through her hair.

"The same. Shape it up a little."

"Ok, let's get you shampooed." I rinsed her hair and squirted gel into my hand.

"Wait." She wrinkled her nose. "That doesn't smell right."

I glanced at the green pool of my favorite herbal shampoo. "You have a preference?"

"Didn't George tell you?"

"No." I wiped the shampoo off my palm with a damp towel. "Which one?"

Her hand flipped again. "Ask George."

George's booth, twice as big as the other booths, stretched across the rear of the salon and provided an incredible view of a charming, wooded area, a gentle creek trickling through it. Enough plants to start a rain forest graced his shelves. A speaker system played waves and seagull cries as I knocked on his entrance. He and another copycat hairdo chatted in animation.

"Yes?" He turned and spotted me, the smile fading from his narrow, pinched face. "Already finished with Brandy?"

"No. I need to know—"

"Excuse me, *cherie*," he sang to his client and escorted me into the hall, his smile fading like my life. "What have you done now?" He crossed his arms. "Brandy tips well, is the sweetest woman on earth, and she'll buy. Don't screw up."

George expected me to push color, gel, mousse, etc. on all my customers. Mom's blue-hairs didn't understand the need—although each week two of her regulars bought something—and my teenage customers "like can't afford it," so George kept sending me Brandys. I did their hair. They didn't complain, but they never rescheduled with me. I'm not charming enough, George claimed.

"She wants a specific shampoo?" I said while I calculated my bank balance. Was it enough to get me out of Dad's house and this salon at the same time? Not even close.

George shoved a pearly pink bottle into my hands and arched an eyebrow at me. "It's only because you brought customers with you that I took you in as an employee rather than renter. If you don't increase your sales, though, I'll find someone who pays me rent and earns those commissions."

Like a chameleon his face transformed into "happy George" as he returned to his booth, his turned back dismissing me with finality.

Armed with the correct shampoo, I returned to Brandy and held up the little pink bottle, waggling it.

She smiled. "That's the one."

When Brandy left, I sold her the shampoo and coordinating conditioner for an exorbitant price.

* * *

Thursday started gloomy and worsened as the morning ticked by. I didn't worry about Brandys on Thursdays because Mom's die-hard blue-hairs came in for their weekly appointments. George hated it. They didn't create the proper image for his reception area.

All morning, I washed and set. And on this gloomy day, I was reminded of those disposable rain bonnets Mom used to wear. Several of my customers carefully secured their settings under one before leaving.

At lunch, I popped open my umbrella and hurried to the bookstore, excited to learn what happened to the debutantes after the golf cart accident.

It would be much easier to buy the book, but I tried bringing a book home when I was ten. A library book—*The Secret Garden*. I'd been in the middle of the chapter where Mary followed Colin's screaming and discovered she was not the only child in the manor house when Dad walked by my room.

He paused in the doorway. "What are you reading?"

"A book my teacher read to us."

"Let me see." He held out his hand.

Clutching the book to my chest, I shook my head.

"Give it to me."

I did, heart pounding in disappointment. "It's a library book. I have to return it."

He glanced at it. "*The Secret Garden*. So they're teaching you to keep secrets? I'll return this to your teacher myself."

After that, my teacher let me borrow any book to read during recess. That's when I decided I wanted to teach. Too bad Dad didn't see any reason to spend my educational fund on four years of college.

"What?" he'd said, surprise crossing his face. "You love to sit in the salon while your mother works. It's honest work."

So, I attended cosmetology school and set up shop in Mom's salon in the basement. I saved every penny, planning to go to college on my own terms. Then I met Steve.

Ten years later, divorced and broke, I returned home to start again.

Excited at my return, Mom announced her retirement, a smile lighting up her face. "You can take over the business. We'll let you run it from here until you get on your feet again."

"But I don't want the business," I'd told my parents.

Quiet settled over the dining room table like the night we'd learned of Uncle Joe's death. The heater ticked as it kicked on and the blowers, shifting the hair on my head, pressed hot air down on me like it had on those dark days after the book banishment.

Dad stared at me for a while and shook his head. "What will you do? You let Steve clean you out."

That's when George hired me. I didn't like him. He tolerated me. If I scrimped, in a year I might have enough to go back to school and work part-time.

I shook out my umbrella before entering the store and headed for the coffee shop, reveling in the combined scents of coffee and books. To the tune of the espresso machine, I pondered my choices. Usually, I ordered the drink on the menu below the one I drank from the previous day—my system to prevent routine and create adventure. Pumpkin Frappuccino. Not good for a cold, dreary day.

"Hi Gail." Megan, the barista glanced up. "So, let's see, you're on the Frappuccinos right? What flavor?"

"Too cold for that." I scanned the menu. "A caramel macchiato?"

Every time I bought one of these concoctions, a twinge of guilt jabbed my conscience. The money should go toward savings, but if I wasn't going to buy books, the least I could do was buy coffee. I paid and waited at the other end of the counter.

"Here ya go." She handed me the cup; heat seeped into my chilled hands. I enjoyed its warmth for a moment, then slid on the cardboard sleeve.

Retreating to my favorite chair—thankfully available—I picked up the tale of Sawyer among the savages of the debutante country club set.

As I finished the book, I overheard a woman ask Reggie, "Do you know who wrote *The Guest Room*?" Reggie headed toward the information desk.

I called after them. "Reggie? Chris Bohjalian. B-O-H something."

The woman turned to me. "Have you read it?"

I nodded. "You can't go wrong with him."

The woman smiled and followed Reggie.

The manager appeared to my left, his attention fixated on me. I got up and made a beeline for the bargain-priced books. Breaking in new employees always frazzled me. Everyone who worked here knew me, but a new employee, manager no less, added tension to the only stress-free moments of my day. Only fifteen minutes before my next client. I needed to grab something cheap to appease the man.

Clearance sported a potpourri of choices, and I scanned the shelves. Thanks to Meals on Wheels, someone could enjoy the books I felt compelled to buy. I picked up a large print copy of *At Home in Mitford*. Its yellow clearance tag read $2.59.

Tucking the book under my arm, I approached the sales counter. As the cashier started to ring up my purchase, the manager stepped in. "I'll take care of this customer."

To my dismay, the cashier nodded and left. Heart thumping, I tried a smile. "Horrible day, isn't it?"

The manager nodded. "Do you come in here every day?"

"Only the days I work."

He frowned at me, the wrinkles deep in his forehead. "The days you work?"

"Yes, it's one of the perks of my job, being so close to so many books."

The manager gave me a probing look. "Your job?"

"George's Salon. Down there." I pointed out the window. "I come in on my lunch hour."

"Oh." His face relaxed. "You're here so often. I thought you meant—never mind." He bagged my purchase. "Too bad you have a job."

"Excuse me?" How could employment be bad news?

"We have an opening, and you know books."

"You want to hire me?" A forbidden thrill slipped down my spine. It was almost sensual. "To work here? With all the books?"

"Of course."

I forced a giddy smile back. "Why?"

"You already help my customers. Thought you might want to get paid."

That was why he'd watched me. He didn't care that I treated his store like a library.

I could spend my days surrounded by the smell of fresh print and the people who loved the written word. Heaven.

My excitement faded fast. George didn't pay well, but it was better than minimum wage. Maybe if I worked weekends.

"Part-time on the weekends?" Could I hide a bookstore job from Dad? Not that he controlled my life, but his house, his rules.

"No, full-time." He shook his head. "I'm sure this doesn't measure up to your income. I've seen some nice cars over there. Probably charge the big bucks, don't you?"

"Yeah," I said. "I do ok." Minimum wage at full-time would not pay enough, and I could never keep it from Dad.

"Too bad. I'm having a hard time finding someone qualified."

"Wish I could help you." I forced a grin of thanks, took my purchase, and trudged into the rain.

Who was I kidding? I'd love it, but Dad would malign that decision every chance he got.

* * *

On Saturday morning I slept until 9am—late for Dad's household. He loved to quote a John Wayne line from *The Cowboys*, "We're burning daylight." I never understood how he justified watching TV shows and movies when books were banned, but it *was* a book that led to Uncle Joe's death.

Mom greeted me as I entered the kitchen. "Well, another country is heard from." I felt nine years old again. She'd been saying that to me every Saturday morning since I could remember.

"Margaret called yesterday. She said you did wonders for her hair. I can't believe she switched to such a simple cut. You must be some saleswoman."

"Tell that to George."

Mom shook her head. "Why do you stay there? The girls tell me he doesn't appreciate you."

I stared at Mom. How many times did I need to explain? "I'm biding my time, Mom. Work isn't easy to come by these days."

I filled a bowl with Frosted Flakes and sat at the white laminate table marred with the scars and scratches of a lifetime of family meals.

"She told me they buy shampoo from you." Mom peered over the rim of her coffee cup at me.

I nodded.

"Why do you let them buy that stuff? You know they don't use it."

"I can't control what they choose to do. Every week, two of them buy something. They rotate."

Mom doesn't understand the sales quota part of my job. She owned her shop and did what she wanted. If she'd wanted to sell products, she could have but never did. I just wish she'd quit asking me about it every week.

Once Mom realized I wasn't going to say more, she sighed and stood up. "Will you pick your father up?"

"Sure. Where?"

Mom frowned and looked around the kitchen in confusion. She slid her hand into the pocket of her bathrobe and withdrew a note; a smile of relief lit her eyes. "Here."

I glanced at the note in Dad's precise handwriting: *Basketball practice starts today. Car's in shop. Pick me up at 11.*

I frowned and turned my attention back to Mom. She ambled down the hall, her motions slow and careful. The hall light revealed several gray strands in her brown hair. She never let it go gray and always kept it perfectly styled. Today, it stuck up at odd angles. I hadn't seen that ratty bathrobe in years, either.

She turned and smiled at me before closing the bedroom door behind her.

* * *

Gravel crunched under the car's tires as I parked beside the ancient brick gym. The one joy Dad and I had shared in my teens was church league basketball. He still coached.

I entered to the hollow echo of balls bouncing on the floor, the squeak of shoes, and the overarching smell of rubber and sweat. Mingled together, they drew me back to simpler days. Dad waved from the bleachers, and I skirted around the girls as they practiced lay-ups. One girl, her hair pulled into a bouncy, red ponytail caught my attention. She exhibited perfect form, and the net swished each time she shot.

"She's good." I nodded in her direction.

Dad squinted. "Yep."

"Why isn't she playing school ball?"

Dad shrugged. "Home schooled."

Unbidden, words itched in the back of my throat. *They probably have books in their house.* Instead, I glanced at my watch. "How much longer?"

In answer, he blew the whistle. Balls bounced one last time, caught by skillful players, and each girl riveted her attention on their coach. "Ok. Enough for today. Pack up and make sure you're here on time next week."

Girls scattered. Two approached Dad.

I stood up. "I'll wait in the car."

With the car's heat blowing on me, I waited. Every few moments a gaggle of players exited the gym. I felt a sudden longing for those days when Saturdays meant practicing lay-ups and drilling for the next game.

Dad walked out alone, pulled the keys from his pocket, locked the door, jiggled the handle, and re-pocketed the keys. All so familiar. I felt fifteen again, hoping he'd relent and let me drive home.

I shook my head. My memories were dragging me backward. Not good. I needed forward motion. "And another job," I muttered as Dad climbed into the car.

"What?" He turned toward me, blue eyes watering.

I studied the ragged frown lines around his mouth, his graying hair. He looked so old. Suddenly, I didn't feel like a child anymore, and an ice pick stabbed my heart. I turned up the heat, trying to ward off the feeling.

"What?" he asked.

"Nothing, Dad." I attempted a smile.

The redhead knocked on the car window, and Dad rolled it down. Cold air crept through the opening, challenging the heater.

"Coach McCall? Did you think about what I asked you?" She blinked at him, youthful hope in her gaze.

Dad's shoulders sagged for a second, then his back straightened. He directed his full attention on the girl. "Joannie, that's between you and your parents. It's your future, not mine."

A relieved smile spread over her face. "Thanks Coach!" Pony-tail swinging, she trotted to her car.

Dad stared after her.

"What was that about?" I said.

He pulled his gaze back to mine. "Joannie? Her parents want

to put her in high school so she can play triple A ball. She might get a college scholarship with the exposure."

Shock pierced my heart. He supported her future? The idea of college for this young girl?

"Don't look so surprised, Gail." Dad tugged his shoulder belt into place. "I'm not that selfish."

I bit my tongue and put the car in drive.

"Before you head home, can we go by the cemetery?" he asked.

I turned left instead of right, mentally checking the date. The anniversary of Uncle Joe's death was yesterday.

The cemetery was deserted. I guess few people wanted to visit their loved ones in the cold. Uncle Joe's stone, simple with just his birth and death dates, nothing personal or flowery, rested half-way across the lawn. Dad didn't linger long, and his eyes watered more when we returned to the car.

"Thanks," he said, his voice quiet.

We were two blocks from home when he shifted and discovered the bag stuck between the console and seat. "What's this?"

My heart lurched when I glanced over—the book I'd bought.

"A book." My voice sounded more nonchalant than I felt.

He pulled it out and smoothed the bag across his lap before laying the book on top of the thin plastic. I watched him out of the corner of my eye as he took the tip of one finger and lifted the front cover. Curiosity and discomfort battled within me while he stared at the book.

A tear splattered on the page.

"Dad?"

He sniffed and wiped his eyes with his sleeve.

"Dad?"

* * *

No school on Monday—a teacher-in-service day, so I worked a packed schedule of teens. The Brandys in the reception area looked down their upturned noses at my, gum-chewing, TikTok-focused clients. Of course, that was the first thing we giggled about when they sat in my chair, then we got down to the business of boys, dates, and cat memes.

At lunch I tried a new book, *Dark Queen* by Faith Hunter. Somehow, I'd managed to keep up with the supply of this long-running series.

When I read the first book, I'd felt an immediate connection with the heroine who took a job with someone she didn't trust or like. Of course, our similarities ended there. Jane spent her days as a kickass heroine fighting vampires, and I was reliving my childhood in an adult world. She carried knives, silver-tipped daggers, and crosses, and I wielded a hair dryer, scissors, and curling iron.

For a brief moment, I imagined Dad finding this book on Saturday. If books were forbidden, vampire books were lecture-worthy.

Then, I remembered Dad crying in my car. He'd said nothing else. When we got home, he'd slid the book in its bag and carried it into the house. This morning, I found it lying on my bedside table, the spine no longer fresh and stiff. I donated it to Meals on Wheels on my way to work.

Sipping a frothy cappuccino, I settled into my comfy, favorite chair.

The story hooked me quickly, so I didn't hear anyone approach until a pair of shoes appeared on the floor in front of me. I looked up into the watery eyes of my father. "Dad?" I flipped the book closed and shoved it between my thigh and the side of the chair.

A quizzical look crossed his face, but instead he glanced down the aisle. I followed his gaze and spotted the manager watching us.

"Thanks." Dad waved. "I found her." He then perched on the edge of a straight-backed chair across from me.

I squirmed under his stare, unsure what this visit could mean. Then I noticed the stack of books propped on his knees.

He gave me an apologetic smile. "Your mom enjoyed that

book you had in your car. She said it was part of a good Christian series. I thought I'd buy her a few more." He cleared his throat and opened the front flap of one of the books. "This one's dedication says: *'For all families who struggle to forgive and be forgiven.'*"

Having delivered the equivalent of a speech, Dad said nothing else, his eyes searching mine.

For a moment, my mind didn't work, I just stared. "I don't understand," I managed to stammer.

"What kind of life is this for you?" He gestured around. "Clandestine trips to the bookstore, ladies' hair?"

I sat back and stared at him. "How did you find me?"

"I know where you spend your lunches." He said this in a calm, matter-of-fact tone, as if we were discussing basketball techniques at a game.

I fought the urge to interrogate him, find out who had loose lips. He didn't appear bothered by my lunchtime pursuits, though, so I focused on his startling question, instead.

What kind of life was this for me? One I hated, stuck in a rut of borrowed books, Brandys, and blue-hairs unable to escape my screwed-up life.

"Gail," Dad said, "I won't pretend I've done things the right way." He leaned forward. "I told Joannie to do what's right for her last Saturday while the person I should have said that to years ago sat beside me."

I rubbed at my nose and sipped my lukewarm cappuccino. What was I supposed to say? Whoopee, I can bring books home? Would that solve my problems? I was still stuck in a hated job and at least a year from financial solvency.

My silence prodded him further. "You need to move out."

Cold shock flooded over me. "What? Because of books?" I jumped to my feet and grabbed my things. My hands shook. I whirled to face him. "Are you serious?"

"Sit down."

His bark still worked, and I obeyed.

"I don't care if you read books. I don't care if you work at that salon either." He chewed his lower lip for a moment. "No. That's not true."

Here we go. I waited for the lecture on evil books and the perfectly good space in the basement for my own salon, and—

"I do care that you work in a job that you hate."

Ok. *Not what I expected.*

Silence worked earlier. Since I had no idea what to say, I waited.

"We're selling the house. Moving into one of those retirement communities. Mom's not herself lately."

I recalled last Saturday, her confusion and the glimpses of gray in her mussed-up hair.

"She's got early stage Alzheimer's."

A chill swept up my arms. "She doesn't," I said even though I knew it was true. I'd seen the signs and ignored them.

In Dad's style, he disregarded my denial. "We have funds set aside for your education."

The twists and turns of his words made my head ache. Why hadn't he mentioned the money before?

He noticed my incredulous look and gave me a bemused smile, again. "Your mom did it, not me. It's quite a sum. She knew you would need it someday but wanted to give you time to figure things out. But now, she's afraid she might—"

His voice cracked, and I reached across the small space and took his cold, wrinkled hand in mine.

He squeezed back. "When she realized she might forget, she told me about the money."

We sat, neither speaking until my cell phone vibrated. I released Dad's hand and glanced at the caller ID.

"Work?" Dad said.

"Yeah. I'm late."

He nodded, a distant look on his face. "Life's too short to do something you don't enjoy." He grunted and pushed on his knees to stand. "I'll see you at home."

I watched his slow progress to the store's front while I answered the phone. "George, I'll be late. Gotta go."

In a daze, I rose.

The manager found me standing there a few minutes later. His voice hummed near me like the background buzz of fluorescent lights.

I jumped when he placed a hand on my arm.

"You Ok?"

I returned to the world and glanced around the store. Somewhere deep inside a little voice prodded me, and I turned and said, "Is that job still available?"

The Magic of the Mountain

The visitor lot held only a few cars when I arrived at Rolling Acres Nursing Home, yet my sister was already there. I parked next to Meredith's hatchback, fighting down the disappointment. She always managed to get there first. Some days, days like today, I wished that wasn't true.

Shouldering my purse, I strode through the sliding doors, hearing the whoosh of compressed air as they whisked shut behind me. I barely noticed the lobby anymore with its wingback chairs upholstered in royal blue and gold—pristine in their disuse. After seven months, the rows of wheelchair-bound residents, faces slack or gazes distant, no longer fazed me. Anything can become normal.

"Help me," a tiny voice called as I passed Miss Liza's room. Today I don't heed her call. Six months ago, the frail voice sucked me in, pulling my attention toward this confused, bed-ridden woman. That was before I'd learned she called out to every person who walked down this hall. Every day, all day long.

Only Mom would get my attention today.

In the dining room, I squeezed between bulky wheelchairs, their geriatric passengers pushed up to tables in the cramped space. Three blue-scrubs-clad CNAs delivered meal trays, weaving between the obstacles in an acrobatic dance. The residents sat listless and unaware of their breakfasts. By dinnertime, this room would resound with each person's unique version of sundowners. I'd witnessed it, the instinctual and surprising reaction to the rising of the moon. Or setting of the sun. You choose.

Meredith sat at the assigned table in her preferred spot, Mom's right side—the side she leaned toward—swirling a spoon in the pureed goo of breakfast. Our mother's lethargic gaze fell on me as I leaned over and kissed her dry, papery cheek. I ran my hand through her straight salt and pepper hair. Before the stroke I had never touched Mom's hair, especially on a Friday after her weekly trip to Vivian's Beauty Parlor. After seven months, I still marveled at the softness of her strands, more salt than pepper these days. She'd aged, looking older than seventy-eight. Had this place aged her or was the culprit the stroke and her body's refusal to function?

"Hi Mom. How's breakfast?"

I pulled a chair up, not expecting a response.

Mom turned her head to follow me, and I took the opportunity to slide her glasses higher on her nose. The smudged lenses bugged me, so I lifted them off her face, fogged them with my breath, and cleaned them on my shirt tail before gently placing them back. "There. That's better."

Meredith shook her head and dredged up a small amount of a yellowish substance on the spoon. "I don't know why you bother. They'll slide down again in a moment." She hovered the spoon near Mom's mouth.

Lips pressed together, Mom turned from the spoon. The irony of this role reversal struck me harder than normal this morning. Probably due to my guilt over my upcoming trip. If mother understood our intention—to clean out and sell the mountain cottage, her favorite place on earth—would she feel betrayed? I loved the mountain as much as her, but nursing homes cost money.

Meredith pressed the spoon against Mom's mouth. Mom reared her head back, teeth clenched. My sister's shoulders slumped.

"Has she eaten anything?"

Meredith frowned and shook her head. "She wouldn't eat supper last night, either."

Feeding Mom could be a challenge some days. But today, alarms triggered in my heart. Was this a sign? "Is she getting sick? Should I stay?"

I could postpone my trip to the cottage. Cleaning it out this week was Meredith's idea, not mine, even though I knew we needed to get it over with. Meredith paused, spoon in hand, to look me in the eyes, promise and determination turning her thin face more serious than normal. "Don't worry. I'll let you know if she gets worse."

Today, the second Friday in June, marked a tradition in our lives. Every year, since my childhood, she and Dad packed us up and headed for a week at the cottage. In those first years after my parents bought the house built into the side of a mountain near Blowing Rock, we filled it with laughter and roamed the Blue Ridge mountains enjoying favorite haunts like Tweetsie Railroad and Grandfather Mountain.

In the last few years, only Mom and I went, content to sit on the mountain, enjoying the peace of its green embrace. This year, I prepared to return alone one last time to say goodbye. To gut the house of our memories.

Sometimes, Mom's oblivion to the world around her was a blessing.

* * *

A few short hours later, I caught my first glimpse of the rolling peak of Grandfather Mountain through my SUV's windshield. It disappeared quickly as clouds descended over it in an ominous expanse of heavy gray. A last ray of sunlight reflected off the Mile

High swinging bridge, rarely visible from Highway 221. Thunder cracked. Rain pounded on the ceiling of the Highlander, drowning out sound. As an added blessing, it drowned out my melancholic thoughts, demanding I focus on driving.

I managed the next few turns, following the brake lights of cars in front of me, then pulled into the Food Lion grocery store parking lot. A few people gathered under the store's awning waiting out the storm, while brave ones exited the store, ducked their heads, and dashed for the haven of their cars. A mother and a toddler ran through the rain, the little boy squealing with delight, stomping in every puddle. When the downpour slowed to a drizzle, I fished out my umbrella.

Water soaked through my tennis shoe as my left foot landed in a large puddle beside the car. Unavoidable. I hopped and skipped across the flooded lot, targeting the shallow spots. When I passed through the automatic doors, cold, recycled air hit my skin, and I longed for a towel as I shivered. My super-absorbent socks squished with every step.

After selecting my meager purchases—orange juice, granola bars, bologna, bread, and coffee—I ventured outside to a different world. Dazzling sunlight glistened across the puddles and sparkling droplets of water rimmed everything like tiny diamonds. It was as if the mountain had paused a moment to grieve with me, then said, "Ok, get on with it, Joy. We're still here and will be here long after you're gone. That's the mountain magic."

Mom and I understood the magic of the mountain. It's why we loved it up here—the clean, crisp air, the timeless immersion in nature, the calm that settled us. I rolled the windows down and let the pure highland ether wash over me. The winding road led me upward, and I guided my SUV through the hairpin turns. The typical thrill of navigating the swift curves eluded me though. A happy retreat did not wait at the end of this road.

Gravel crunched under my tires as I pulled into the drive in front of the cottage. The small house stood on stilts buried in the side of the mountain, trees towering around it. Built of dark-gray wood, it's fogged windows looked deserted, empty. New patches of green moss grew on the roof. Something else to think about this week.

Stuffy, warm air hit me as I fumbled the door open.

The large living room spread before me, its shuttered windows waiting to invite in the mountain's vista. I dropped my bags in the entry and crossed to those windows, drew the blinds open to let in the afternoon sun. The cranks to the windows stuck, but with some grunting and effort, the windows squeaked open to admit a breeze.

Hands on my hips, I surveyed the room, my gaze falling on the chairs gone soft and faded from years of use and the kitchen to my left, sparse and unusually clean.

The house rang with an impossible emptiness without her. Without Mom.

For the first time in my life, I put my things in the master bedroom. It felt wrong, but no reason to use the upstairs when it wasn't necessary. I placed my bologna and juice in the fridge and stood staring at the sparse supplies. Mom would have filled the kitchen to overflowing with more food than she or I could eat. The refrigerator door whispered shut as I wandered away hungry for something besides food.

With a few hours of daylight left, I dragged packing boxes and tape out of my trunk and started dismantling our lives in the two upstairs bedrooms. After a quick bologna sandwich at nine, I collapsed into bed.

In the middle of the night, another storm blew through billowing the curtains on the sliding door in the master bedroom. As a child, I would have seen ghosts in those folds, but I only felt the sigh of the wind and the tears of the sky. As thunder rumbled in the distance, I gave up on sleep and went over my checklist for cleaning out the cottage. Each room's items were catalogued to be packed and shipped to family members, the cottage emptied of Mom once and for all.

Just before dawn, sleep finally overtook me.

* * *

The clattering of pots and pans from the neighbor's cottage below ours woke me. Pages of my spreadsheets fluttered to the floor as I threw back the covers and crossed to the window. Bright sunlight filtered through the green leaves of the trees. I smiled at the lush growth around the deck, inhaling the fragrance of wind, sun, rain-soaked soil, and leaves. The aroma of bacon mingled with the breeze.

My mouth watered. I should have bought bacon.

Pulling the sliding door closed, I paused, confused by the sound of a pot clanging against the sink in the kitchen, the rush of water from a faucet. The bacon smell still hovered in the air.

From inside the cottage.

I waited, standing still, second-guessing the sounds.

Silence.

I shrugged and bent to tidy the bed.

But the voice I thought I'd never hear again came to me through the walls of the cottage: *Try to remember, da da-ta-di-da-ta.*

The hair on my neck stood up. Mom always sang while working in the kitchen. I stumbled toward the door, but the voice had already faded like an echo from the past. Wishful thinking, that's all. Nothing but memories.

I dug a pair of old Calvin Klein jeans and a faded Red Cross T-shirt out of my suitcase.

I paused, again, like a rabbit that senses the hawk but can't pinpoint the danger, at the faint clink of a spoon against a cup.

Silence.

I turned to the window beside the bed. Open? No. That wouldn't explain the song, anyway.

I breathed a sigh and sat down on the bed. "Get yourself together, Joy."

Mom always said I had more imagination than the rest of the family combined.

Then I heard the sucking sound of the refrigerator door being opened, the gurgle of a coffee maker. The singing started again.

La-da-ti-dada, then fol-low, follow, follow, fol-low.

I licked my lips, my tongue picking up the salty flavor of a tear trickling down my cheek. Shaky hands wiped away the tear. I jerked on my clothes in a hurry, hands trembling, fumbling with the zipper. Mom, also, said I sensed the spirit of the mountain more than most. Mountain magic, she called it. Of course, she didn't tell me this as a child, only later when spectral presences could not be blamed on childish nightmares.

I inched forward, avoiding creaking floorboards, straining for a sound. The house lay quiet again.

It's nothing. I'm sure it's nothing.

But one couldn't be too careful when alone. I grabbed my cell phone, prepared to dial 9-1-1 if something unwanted waited on the other side of the door.

Clink. Clink. Clink. Three swirls in her coffee. That's how Mom added sugar.

Every nerve in my body screamed at me to do something. Open the door. Climb under the bed. Call the nursing home. Act rational and march in there. No one is there. It's your active imagination playing tricks on you.

I cracked the door open. A light burned in the kitchen. Had I left it on?

I tiptoed down the short hall.

"Good morning, Joy." Mom smiled up at me from the breakfast table, a plate of bacon, eggs, and grits before her, a slice of buttered toast balanced on the plate's rim like every Saturday morning in my memories. Her glasses sat straight on her nose, no smudges. Her hair, more pepper now, curled around her ears in Vivian's classic styling.

I went cold.

"I was hoping you'd get up in time," she said.

What did that mean? Was this vision momentary, about to fade? I blinked, swallowed, noticed I wasn't breathing and inhaled, smell the flower, and exhaled, blow out the candle. Smell the flower, blow out the candle.

"In time?" My voice squeaked, but she didn't appear to notice.

"Before your breakfast gets cold. Eggs and grits aren't worth eating if they're cold." A smile of delight crossed her face as she sat back and sipped her coffee. "Isn't it a beautiful morning?"

When had I last seen that smile? Seven, maybe eight months ago?

"Um. Mom?" My voice sounded weak and muffled like I spoke from a walled-off compartment. Probably thanks to the blood racing through my body trying to keep up with the tempo of my pounding heart.

She tilted her head to the left, such a familiar gesture. "Yes?"

I stared at her, afraid to speak, afraid to move, afraid she'd dissolve before my eyes.

"Honey, are you ok?" She put down her cup and leaned forward.

The concern on her face broke me. I rushed to her and wrapped my arms around her body, expecting to fall through this vision like some horrible B-rate movie. She felt solid, real, not weak and fragile. Her smell, White Shoulders powder not the nursing home's institutional stink laced with urine, enveloped me. "You're here," I whispered into her hair.

She patted my hand. "Of course I am. Where else would I be?"

Good question. What did she—*if* she was she—know? Could she really be here, solid, alert, capable, eating breakfast and drinking coffee?

Tears threatened, and I backed away, not wanting her to see. I turned and bustled into the kitchen, stealing furtive glances to reassure me she was still there.

So much of what I'd missed since the stroke—her smile, her happy singing, that tilt of her head. Could this be real? Tears won the battle, blinding me as I reached for a plate and spooned up grits and eggs then added bacon.

I grabbed a paper towel and wiped my eyes, blew my nose. I had to pull myself together. Was I still asleep? Going crazy?

It seemed cliché, but I put down the plate and pinched myself. Hard. An inch of arm skin squeezed between thumb and forefinger. It hurt. She remained at the table, piling into her eggs and grits.

Shoulders squared, I turned to face this apparition. Maybe the magic of the mountain offered one last chance for me. It didn't matter why she was here, what mattered was she was.

While we ate, she told stories of her childhood. Stories I'd heard before—the time she got measles and her family was quarantined, the Christmas all of us kids got sick, how Dad courted her before they married, the day she and Dad found the cottage. Time ticked by, and I didn't stir from the table, afraid the magic might fade.

In the middle of this, as I sat marveling at the play of muscles on her face, the quick smile, laughter, the ability to move her hands, my phone rang. Meredith.

By now she'd know Mom was missing. I didn't want to share her, though. I excused myself and crossed to the other side of the room to answer, my breakfast solidifying like concrete in my gut. "Hey. How's Mom today?"

"Maybe you should come back." Meredith's voice trembled. "We can't wake her this morning."

I glanced back at Mom. Could I leave to visit a shell when the filling, the insides that made her our mom, sat across the room from me? "Have you spoken to the doctor?"

Meredith huffed. "We're waiting. I'm sorry I made you go up there. Please come back."

I ran my hand through my hair. "She's here."

"I know, I know." Meredith's voice cracked with sympathy. "I shouldn't have let you go up there alone to face all those memories. Come home. We'll handle it together once we know what's going on with Mom."

I heard what she didn't say: "We'll do this after Mom dies. This illness could be the one that tips the scales toward the end."

I had to stall. I needed to stay. "I've made good headway up here, but sure, I'll come back. But let's wait until you talk to the doctor. I'll come if she thinks I should."

Meredith sighed, but agreed.

As I hung up, Mom rose from the chair and nodded toward the upstairs. "I know you have work to finish. I'm going to rest for a while."

I started after her. "It can wait. I'd rather spend the day with you."

She kissed me on the cheek, her warm fingers on my shoulder. "Later." She ambled into the master bedroom.

I stared after her until I heard the bed creak under her weight. Then I turned to clear the breakfast dishes from the table.

The kitchen was spotless. Empty. No pot of grits, no frying pan in the sink, everything like I'd left it the night before. Yet, I held two plates in my hands, smeared yellow with egg trails and spotted with pebbles of hardened grits.

The dishes clattered when I dropped them on the counter. I yanked open the refrigerator. My breakfast did an uneasy swirl in my stomach, threatening to come up. Only bologna and juice on the shelves. Where had the eggs and bacon come from? The trashcan remained empty, no egg cartons or bacon packages tossed there.

On tiptoe, I approached the master bedroom. The door sat ajar, and I eased it open.

No Mom.

I rushed into the room and searched the closet, the bathroom, the deck. No Mom.

With shaking hands, I picked up my phone and called my husband.

His calm, deep voice picked up on the other end—voicemail.

"Hi, it's me. Um, I just wanted to hear your voice. It's weird here, but...never mind. I love you." I hung up. With the recent storms, the insurance claims business kept him busy. My message probably sat in the middle of several homeowners' calls insisting he get to them faster, sooner. I dropped the phone on the bed, falling in a heap beside it.

* * *

I woke around noon and stretched to relieve the kinks from sleeping on the floor. Stretching my neck left and right, I climbed to my feet and wandered back into the kitchen. Still no sign of Mom or her preparation of our breakfast.

"Mom?" I called out in a soft voice, unsure why I felt the need to be quiet.

Nothing.

I wandered through the cottage, finding everything as I'd left it the night before. It had to be a dream, the ghosts of the old mountain magic getting to me.

Grabbing a granola bar, I climbed the stairs and continued packing.

By dinner time, I'd finished the extra bedrooms. That left the master, living area, and kitchen. Dinner was a bologna sandwich and chips. Exhausted, I collapsed in an old chair, the fabric a faded, burnt-orange, and clicked on the TV.

An evening storm rumbled in the distance, and I curled into a ball in the chair, remote in hand, clicking through the channels, seeing nothing but Mom's smile this morning.

As the storm grew closer, the cable flickered, then went out. I called it an early night.

My night passed in a dreamless coma.

A woodpecker attacking the deck woke me. I dragged out of bed, muscles aching from my odd naps yesterday. Heart aching from the memory of an all-too-real apparition, I checked my phone. A message from Meredith told me all was fine. Not to worry.

Showered, and dressed in a pair of old Levi's and a Save the Ta-Ta's T-shirt, I straightened my shoulders and listened for singing. None.

The house felt comfortably empty as I ventured into the kitchen to make coffee and grab another granola bar. My breakfast of champions finished, I tackled the bookshelves cluttered with vacation reading, board games, puzzles, and a myriad of knick-knacks that had migrated to the cottage from Mom's house over the years. Behind one of the books, I found a key.

"So that's where that was."

I shrieked and whirled around. Mom sat on the sofa, a book in her lap.

"What?"

"That key. I lost it years ago."

Dumbfounded, I stared at her. She sat where she'd spent most summer mornings, reading a paperback book, probably a mystery.

"There's a shed underneath the house. Behind the water heater. It opens it." She turned a page. "You'll need to clean it out, too, but I imagine there's not much there. I haven't been down there in ages."

If the key had been missing for years, then what surprise, besides my mother's presence, awaited me under this house?

"Aren't you ready for lunch?" she asked, setting the book aside. "I'm starving."

I laid my hand over my stomach. Moments earlier, food hadn't appealed to me, but now? I nodded.

She flashed that joyous smile again, a chuckle following it. "I thought so. You always were one to get caught up in work and miss a meal. How about a pizza?"

A pizza sounded great. "I didn't buy any."

She rose and picked up her purse from the kitchen counter, pulling some bills out of it. Where had those come from?

"Call Antonio's for carry out. This should cover it."

I folded the worn bills in my hand. They felt real. If I left, would she be here when I returned? I hesitated. I couldn't just leave. "Why don't you come with me? We'll eat there?"

A frown of confusion crossed her face, the expression more like the glazed one I'd become used to over the last few months. "I don't think so. I'd rather stay here."

She sat back down and picked up the book.

I hovered.

"Joy," the reprimand in her voice so familiar I expected my full name to trip over her lips. "I'll be fine right here. Go. I'm famished."

Unable to silence my worries, I followed her command. It's funny how parents keep that hold over us.

After placing the order and washing up, I drove down the mountain at breakneck speed to pick up the pizza. On impulse, I bought a bottle of her favorite wine.

When I pushed open the cottage's door a scant twenty-three minutes later, she still sat in the chair where I'd left her. A sigh of relief escaped my lips, and I sagged against the doorframe trying to calm the nervous pounding of my heart.

"I turned the oven on in case it got cold." She bookmarked her place and came into the kitchen. "I miss pizza."

I nodded, unsure how to respond to that revelation. Could she really be here? Aware? Sharing the thoughts her stroke-damaged mind couldn't?

I popped the pizza in the oven. The aromas of pepperoni and tomato sauce filled the small house, and I breathed them in, appreciating what I couldn't on my frantic ride back up the mountain.

We sat at the table devouring the pizza and sipping wine. We ate every last bite and drank the whole bottle. Her enjoyment of the cabernet squeezed my heart. Simple pleasures once taken for granted now denied her in the nursing home.

I studied her over the rim of my almost empty wine glass. Was she here or there?

Did it matter?

She fiddled with the key I'd laid on the table after its discovery. "You know, the shed didn't used to have a lock. We got it because of you."

"Me?" I sat back in surprise.

A tender smile tipped the corners of her lips. "Yes. That year we let you invite some friends up here. You remember? Cassie and Pam came with you. You girls played games upstairs and raced around this house like it was your own private playground."

I nodded, a vague memory of the trip in the back of my mind. Cassie and Pam had long since disappeared from my life, but I did remember late night giggling sessions and wandering around the mountainside behind the cottage.

"One day, we called you for lunch—y'all were upstairs playing a game, we thought—but you didn't answer. We looked everywhere for you, panicking, calling the police. No one could find you."

I straightened in my seat.

"I don't know what made me check the shed. We never used it, but that's where I found the three of you, hovered over a pile of rocks. You'd gone on a treasure hunt, sure you'd find gold."

"You would think I'd remember that." I picked up the key.

"You don't?" She peered at me in surprise. "Well, the three of you went on and on about gold and magic in the mountainside for the rest of that day."

"Gold and magic. I could use some of that today."

"You have all you need right here." A sad smile crossed her face as she rose from the table. "I need to rest. Go on with your work."

Jumping to my feet, I reached for her. "No wait."

Her smile broadened. I would never tire of seeing this evidence of her happiness again. She patted my hand. "Joy, I'm still here. Don't worry."

I remained frozen in place as she wandered into the bedroom. The bed creaked, and the house fell silent.

I bit my lip. Was she still here? Two wine glasses, a pizza box, and two plates said yes, but...

I crept to the door.

The bedroom was empty.

Sorrow seeped through me, and I settled in the chair she'd sat in moments earlier, my fingers brushing the pages of the book she'd been reading, *The Physician* by Noah Gordon. I skimmed the back cover, one line stabbing me in the heart: *as he matures, his strange gift—an acute sensitivity to impending death—never leaves him, and he yearns to become a healer.*

Was there a message in this or did I want there to be one?

I opened to her bookmark and started reading. Within a couple of pages, I drifted off to sleep.

When I awoke, the paperback lay in a heap in the floor. The last light of the day shone through the windows. Resigned, and feeling older than my fifty years, I picked up the book and laid it on the end table. The key sat on the table, and I thought about checking the closet, but the thought of going down there at night prickled the hair on my neck.

Packing still needed to be done, anyway. I packed up the rest of the living room that evening and most of the kitchen, leaving out the few items I needed for meals. After a brief call home, unable to sleep, I started on the master bedroom.

Mom's scent, White Shoulders, wafted from the underwear drawer when I pulled it open. I hesitated over the contents, personal pieces that concealed her in ways that the ever-present hospital gown didn't.

With a sigh, I shoved them in a trash bag. No one wanted used underwear, I don't care how desperate you were. She only kept a few changes of clothes in the cottage, so it didn't take long to empty the closet and drawers into bags to donate. I'd packed up the books and knickknacks from her nightstand with the ones from the living room earlier.

That left the bathroom. Most of that went in the trash.

Meredith called as I surveyed the empty drawers and walls. "How's it going?" Her voice resonated compassion. We had cleaned out Mom's main house together, so she knew how the experience laid bare your soul.

I leaned against the wall and slid to the floor. "Almost done. I can't believe what's left of her life fits into a few boxes."

We sat in silence a moment, each lost with her own approach to the decline of our vibrant mother.

Memories of Mom's visit haunted me as I asked, "How is she today?"

"Quiet now, but she perked up last night and this morning. Then she shut down after lunch time. She's asleep now. If I didn't know better, I'd say she was drunk during lunch."

"What?" I lurched upright, running a hand through my hair. "Drunk? Why?"

"She had this goofy grin on her face and smiled a lot but with less effort. The nurse commented on it, too. It was kind of funny." Meredith laughed on the other end, the sound reminding me how laughter helped us see some days through.

The idea that what I saw up here reflected in our mother's behavior at the nursing home confused me. *What was going on?*

"Did you know there's a locked shed under the house?" I asked.

"Yes. You might have to get a locksmith to open it. Mom hasn't seen the key in years. It's probably full of junk to be thrown away."

"I think I found the key. I forgot the shed was down there."

That night, I dreamed over and over again about the shed. Each time I opened the door, something lurched out. First it was a skeleton, then a horde of rats, another time, three small girls, curled in blankets, turned blue from freezing in their sleep.

I woke in the morning, exhausted and determined to face the shed and any other spirits remaining in this house.

Mom was a no-show as I ventured under the house. Narrow

stairs wound down the steep slope beside the cottage. Half of the underside of the house remained open to the world, the other half was lodged into the mountainside. The water heater sat in a fenced-in square next to the main support holding up the house. Behind it was a small shed-like closet, the door grayed from exposure.

The key fit. It grated against the metal of the lock and resisted my efforts to turn it. Feet braced, I grasped it with both hands and twisted. Sweat trickled down my forehead as I tried again and again. Finally, the weathered metal groaned and gave way.

The door creaked open. A musty, earthen smell wafted out as I fumbled for a light switch. Faint illumination from a single bare bulb revealed a few cracked flowerpots covered in dust and cobwebs. Dust motes floated in the scant light. The far wall held a dilapidated shelf, a shadow of something resting on it. I turned on my phone's flashlight and crept toward the wall, glancing at the ceiling and dirt floor for any creepy-crawly inhabitants. Had my friends and I really chosen this filthy spot to count our treasures?

The shadow turned out to be a rusted metal lockbox with a three-dial combination lock.

"Great. Another lock." I dusted the box off, my head turned to avoid the swirl of sneeze-guaranteed grime. The box felt light. When I shook it, something shifted inside with a dull clunk.

"Why would Mom leave this down here?" I muttered as I tried numbers Mom used for almost everything—her phone number, birthdate, wedding date. The lock did not yield.

I glanced around the shadowed closet. "Mom?"

Birds continued to sing outside.

I carried the box into the daylight. "I hope you show up, Mom, or I'll have to break open this box."

Several birds flew into the sky, crying out in alarm. As I trudged up the stairs, nothing else joined me.

I sat at the table, nursing a cup of coffee and trying different number combinations for the rest of the morning. When Mom failed to appear and noon approached, I loaded the car with boxes to be mailed or dropped at Goodwill. Before I left, I stood in the doorway. "Mom?"

My voice echoed in the empty cottage.

A hollow feeling settled in my chest as I disposed of what was left of Mom's worldly goods. Afterward, I sat in my car at an intersection, trying to convince myself to head back to the deserted cottage. Instead, I drove toward Boone. One last supper at the Dan'l Boone Inn beckoned me.

Even though the hour was early for dinner, a line snaked out of the two-story white house onto the rocking chair porch. I joined the line, and others soon followed. The family-style meals always drew a crowd.

A couple with two young boys stood behind me in the line. They chattered about their day at Tweetsie Railroad. I smiled at my own memories of the amusement park as I eavesdropped. Soon the boys started talking about their plans for the next few days. When they didn't mention Grandfather Mountain, I succumbed to my compulsion to share.

"Tomorrow should be a clear day. You should try Grandfather before the rain returns."

The mother smiled at me. "We weren't sure about the kids. There's a swinging bridge up there. Is it safe?"

I eyed her rambunctious boys, grinning when they rolled their eyes over their mother's caution. "It's perfectly safe," I said, then turned a parental stare on the children, "as long as you follow the rules. You don't want to miss out on the Mile High Bridge, do you?"

As the line inched forward, the boys peppered me with questions about Grandfather, Linville Caverns, gem mining and other tourist landmarks. They were from Chicago, so everything about the Blue Ridge Mountains enchanted them.

As we approached the hostess stand, I told them, "At least, you're getting one of the must-do activities covered tonight by eating here."

I'd been smelling the aroma of fried chicken and ham biscuits for twenty minutes, so the recommendation was heartfelt. No trip to the mountains was complete without a meal at the Dan'l Boone Inn.

The hostess frowned when I said, "One."

"We've only got large tables open right now. It could be a while."

A solitary diner posed a seating nightmare during tourist season. I nodded my acceptance while calculating how late I could wait and still make it back up the mountain before dark. When I'd left, I hadn't planned to be gone all day. Returning to a dark house, one where my mother popped in without warning, wasn't an ideal way to end this difficult day.

The hostess looked past me to the family behind. "How many in your party?"

"Four," the boys announced.

"Five," their mother said. She turned to me. "If you want to join us?"

As we waited for our food, I kept the conversation light, focused on tourist info. The only time I mentioned Mom was when the ham biscuits arrived. "My mom loves these. Eat them while they're hot. They won't bring extras like everything else."

Turns out country ham didn't appeal to my Chicago friends, so I left the restaurant that night with contraband—three ham biscuits swaddled in napkins and tucked inside my purse.

The sun was beginning to set as I pulled up to the cottage. A light glowed in the windows, and I held my breath as I peered through the window.

She sat at the table, the lockbox in front of her. When I entered, she glanced up, then returned to contemplating the box. "I'd forgotten about this box. Where did you find it?"

I fished the ham biscuits out of my purse and set them before her. "In the shed. It was the only thing in there."

A smile spread over her face as she unfolded the napkins. "You went to the Inn." The smile faded for a moment. "I guess I'll never go there again."

A tear glistened in her eye.

I sat down next to her, my hand covering hers. "Mom? Can I ask you something?"

She nodded. "I wondered when you would. I've been waiting."

"Are you?" I paused and thought for a moment. Could I really have this conversation? I needed to know, so I asked, "Are you really here?"

"Yes." She pinched a piece of the biscuit off and placed it on her tongue like it was a communion wafer. "Thank you for these. I miss real food."

Real food. Ok, I'd start with that.

"Are you in the nursing home?"

Her brown eyes lifted to mine, their light still vibrant unlike when I saw her before heading to the mountains. "Yes. In a way."

"But how?"

She shook her head and turned to stare at the setting sun, its fire turning the world pink and orange as it gave way to darkness.

When the shadows took over the mountainside, she turned back to me. "I think the answer is in this box."

"Do you remember the combination? I couldn't open it."

"You'll know it when the time is right. Then, you can open the box. Until then, promise me you won't try."

"But—"

"Promise me."

"If that's what you want. I'll wait."

She pinched off another piece of biscuit and chewed it. "I do miss food."

I had tried her pureed meals, surprised at the decent flavor. Of course, texture made a huge difference. "Is it that bad?"

"No," she said. "I don't think I know when I'm there."

"What do you mean?"

She finished off the last biscuit and smiled. "I'd explain if I could." Her cool fingers caressed my cheek and wiped away a tear

I didn't know I'd spilled. "I know my girls are there and watching over me. That's all that matters."

"I'm sorry, Mom."

"Don't be. I'm enjoying our time together. Let's not focus on what we can't fix."

"Do you want me to bring Meredith up here? I feel guilty that I haven't told her."

Mom has several laughs. This one was unrestrained, a loud bark of laughter followed by a snort. I think it's my favorite.

"Honey, Meredith would never admit to seeing me. She'd decide you're crazy and worry about you from this day on. Don't feel guilty. She's getting the time she needs with me in other ways."

Relief flooded my mind, and I relaxed for the first time since coming to the mountain. "This is what I needed?"

"Of course. Why else would I be here?" She rose and went to the sofa, patting the seat beside her. "Let's watch TV."

We sat on the sofa, leaning into each other, a light blanket draped over our legs. I burrowed closer and took her hand. What we watched didn't matter. We were together.

I must have drifted off to sleep, because she woke me with a gentle nudge. "Joy, I'm waning. This time, I don't think I can come back." She glanced around the room, now stripped of everything that made it her cottage. "There's nothing to draw me. In the morning, open the box."

Her words poured adrenaline's fire through my veins. "Wait. No." I glanced at the box. "I don't even know—"

When I turned back, I sat on the sofa alone. She was gone

I cried.

The phone woke me around six am. I rubbed the sleep from my eyes and groped for it on the coffee table. "Hello?"

"Hi honey, did I wake you?" Scott's voice embraced me the way it always did early in the morning.

"Yes, but I need to get up. A lot to do before I leave today."

"You want me to come up and help you load everything?" he

asked. "I'm ready to head out if you want. Bring you Starbucks, too."

I moaned at the thought. The mountain had coffee shops, but not Starbucks. "No. I just need to load a few boxes and drop the key off at the realtor's. We're going to try to sell it furnished, so no need to cart off anything big."

After a few more moments of catching up, we said our good-byes. I rose from the couch, folding the blanket. My gaze fell on the box. Mom said I'd know when it was time. The clock read 6:15. Today was June 15, the anniversary of the day they bought the cottage. Could it be?

I spun the dials to 6-1-5 and held my breath.

The box opened.

Inside was an envelope with my name written in my mother's spidery handwriting.

It held a small stone and a postcard of the mountain. I flipped over the card. On the back she had written: *The mountain magic dwells in your soul. No matter where you go, keep a piece of it with you, and I'll be there.*

The stone was nothing remarkable, just a piece of rock, but it radiated warmth as I held it. Could it be part of my childhood treasure?

By eight, I was on the road. The house, empty of Mom, held nothing for me anymore.

The lockbox with the stone was nestled in between the boxes meant for me and Meredith.

It was lunchtime when I drew near to home. Without thought, I drove past our neighborhood and headed for Rolling Acres.

Meredith sat in the small dining room in the same place she had sat on the day I'd left, Mom beside her, another plate of pureed goo on the table.

Mom looked at me with listless eyes, and I forced my mind to recall the intent gaze she gave me the night before. I held the stone and squatted down beside her, taking her cold, useless hand in mine, wrapping her fingers around the stone.

For a brief moment, a light flashed in her eyes, and she turned to me.

"Was it you?" I asked.

And she squeezed my hand.

About the Author

Barbara V. Evers is the author of THE WATCHERS OF MONIAH epic fantasy trilogy. From the Dark Corner of South Carolina, she crafts fantasy stories with strong women matriarchies and unusually gifted animals. I mean, seriously, she has telepathic giraffes in her trilogy! A two-time Best Fantasy Novelist, she's won several awards for her writing over the years.

A supporter and advocate for giraffe conservation, when she's not writing, Barbara is teaching adults how to communicate or herding her husband, grandchildren, and her rescue dog, Roxy everywhere they need to be (but don't tell them).

To learn more about Barbara and subscribe to her newsletter, go to www.BarbaraVEvers.com.

Also by Barbara V. Evers

The Watchers of Moniah Trilogy:

The Watchers of Moniah
The Watchers in Exile
The Watchers at War

If you enjoyed these stories...

...check out the first book in Barbara V. Evers' award-winning epic fantasy trilogy.

From *The Watchers of Moniah, Book 1*

Prologue

Queen Chiora of Moniah leaned back on her throne, her gaze steady on the traitor, Maligon. The sight of her once truest friend tightened the knot in her stomach. The gathered nobles hushed as he strode past them, head held high, escorted by two women of the queen's Watchers. The heat in the air lay thick as a blanket. The silence matched it. Chiora resisted the urge to shift in her seat as sweat pooled inside her uniform, the leathers chosen over ceremonial dress to remind him she was a soldier, not just a figurehead.

Sunlight poured into the open courtyard and radiated across the landowners' formal robes of glimmer cloth, creating a rainbow of iridescent color around them. Normally, she enjoyed the play of the sunlight on their clothing, but today she couldn't. Today, they waited to witness the sentencing of the man who dared bring destruction to the kingdoms.

The Watchers and Maligon came to a stop below Chiora's Seat of Authority. He wore the plain clothes of a prisoner but still stood tall and well-muscled, his dark hair tied back in a fighter's tail. His black eyes once caressed her in love, but now they radiated hatred so pure it shimmered in the air.

"Maligon," Queen Chiora spoke, her voice firm and strong, "you betrayed me. And so you betrayed us all. And for what? Power you didn't need."

Maligon's black eyes didn't blink. He sneered at her. His injured hand twitched. She watched it with dispassionate interest. He'd never wield a sword again, a satisfying bit of knowledge even if he was about to die.

She took a focused breath, centering her mind and soul. "I sentence you to wear the oxen head into the desert."

A low murmur of approval hummed through the onlookers.

Maligon continued to stare venom at her as she gestured to the Watchers. "Take him from my sight."

The two Watchers, dressed in the tanned leather tunics and leggings of Chiora's all-female guard, escorted Maligon from the hall. He walked between the tall soldiers, head still held high.

Chiora drew a deep breath, the tension in her muscles easing as the air spread into her chest and throughout her body. She took another breath, and another. With each controlled inhalation, she drew her focus inward, preparing to bear witness as her soldiers carried out Maligon's sentence outside the walls of her fortress. The sentence would finish him. The heat, even this far from the desert bordering her lands, baked the air.

As her breathing settled into a steady rhythm, she sent a tendril of thought into the telepathic link with Ju'latti, her royal giraffe. Tension slid from her neck and shoulders as the noble beast embraced the connection. Through this link, Chiora looked through the animal's eyes and saw a throng of tribal villagers gathered outside the walls of the fortress. They stood near the horses where the soldiers led Maligon, but not too close. She couldn't blame them after the devastation the traitor and his followers wreaked on their lands.

Two Watchers lashed Maligon to the back of a donkey, securing the bindings so neither traitor nor beast could dislodge the man. Then they handed a large skin bucket to a squad of First Soldiers, the male branch of Moniah's military. At the edge of the desert, the soldiers would remove a water-soaked oxen head from the bucket and secure it over Maligon's.

Chiora squinted at the sky. The sun, now a short distance above the horizon, promised a scorching day. Just before it reached its pinnacle, the First Soldiers would place the suffocating weight of the oxen head over Maligon's. A few hours later, the soldiers would stab the donkey's rump, driving it farther into the desert. In the heat, the wet oxen head would dry and conform to Maligon. Suffocation would kill him long before the donkey collapsed from exhaustion.

And if he survived? Chiora shook her head. No one had survived this sentence in hundreds of years.

* * *

Want more? Get *The Watchers of Moniah* to discover:
A Warrior Princess
  A Dying Queen
    A Traitor Returned from the Dead
      & A Shocking Deathbed Command
        Oh, and telepathic giraffes. You **CAN'T** forget the giraffes!

Made in the USA
Middletown, DE
07 April 2024

52548501R10071